A CAULDRON OF UNCANNY DREAMS

DONALD FIRESMITH

For Gabby

Enjoy!

Donald Firesmith

A Cauldron of Uncanny Dreams

By Donald Firesmith

Copyright 2021-2022 by Donald G. Firesmith

Second Edition: April 2023

10 9 8 7 6 5 4 3 2

This book is a work of fiction. Any similarities to real people, living or dead, are purely coincidental. All characters and events in this work are figments of the author's imagination.

1. Paranormal 2. Fantasy 3. Occult 4. Horror

Purchase autographed books by contacting the author at:

Magical Wand Press

20 Bradford Avenue

Pittsburgh, PA 15205

https://donaldfiresmith.com

Edited using AutoCrit™, Grammarly™, and ProWritingAid™

Book cover by Pamela C. Rice

Interior design by Donald Firesmith

TABLE OF CONTENTS

Her Mother's Eyes	1
The Collector	2
Grandma Buford's Birthday	12
The Farmer's Daughter	16
The Haunting of the Ederescu House	31
Madam Kaldunya's Dolls	52
Billy the Arsonist	66
A Mother's Grief	74
A Mother's Love	78
The Governess	129
Hexendorf	139
Revenge	158
The Vow	165
Homage to H. P. Lovecraft	166

HER MOTHER'S EYES

She has her mother's eyes.
She keeps them in the back of her freezer
with her father's hands and her husband's heart.
She thinks of them often…
And smiles.

Author's Comments

The idea for this tiny gem came to me when I was rereading the Harry Potter novels, in which people constantly remind Harry that he has "his mother's eyes." In it, I had two goals: to turn the meaning of the phrase on its head and to distill the concept into the most compact form possible. What I especially like about this story is the questions it raises. What are the symbolisms of her mother's eyes, her father's hands, and her husband's heart? What did the mother see? What did the father do, and what was the husband's heartfelt emotion?

THE COLLECTOR

Margery McElroy was a collector. In fact, all her friends were collectors. Janet Wilson, who lived across the street, collected salt and pepper shakers from around the world. Harriet Miller lived two streets over and had a collection of hundreds of ceramic frogs, while Margery's friend, Lisa Howard, collected miniature paintings of butterflies.

But Margery had never been very interested in her friends' collections, not really. Of course, she would never give the slightest hint of her boredom with frogs or painted butterflies. When she visited her friends, Margery would listen to them prattle on and on about their recent finds, smiling and nodding approvingly when they presented their newest prizes. But she only humored the others so that when she invited them over, they would 'ooh' and 'ah' in envious admiration as she regaled them with her latest treasure, a rare discovery in perfect condition without the slightest crack or chip.

Margery collected miniature ceramic houses and buildings of all kinds. She started years ago with an inexpensive Christmas village, and her collection rapidly expanded from there. Soon, she was adding small snow-covered trees and tiny figurines of Christmas carolers to a wintry village that had grown into a small town covering her entire dining room table. The following October, she added a Halloween town with half a dozen haunted houses to her Christmas collectibles. The next spring, she added an entire coastline of porcelain lighthouses. By summer, it ceased to matter what it was, expensive or cheap, finely crafted or the most crudely constructed, just so long as it was something new to add to her ever-expanding collection.

Since her husband passed four years earlier and her children were all grown and in homes of their own, Margery filled her empty days and empty house with small ceramic buildings of every shape and kind. Her son's old room celebrated Christmas all year long, while her daughter's bedroom held a miniature Halloween haunted by hundreds of minuscule ghosts and monsters of every kind. Not a single surface in any room remained that had not been transformed into a landscape of tiny towns and diminutive villages. As the months went by, her guests grew to feel like Gulliver in a porcelain land of Lilliputians.

Depending on the time of the year, every Saturday would find Margery and her friends trawling the antique shops, flea markets, yard sales, and estate sales. On Sundays, while the others were in church, Margery would religiously drive to nearby towns. She would look for out-of-the-way places where she could find that one-of-a-kind treasure that would force her to rearrange her rooms and perhaps even move an older find into a closet, or worse yet, a neatly labeled box in her overstuffed attic.

It was on just such a Sunday that she discovered *Aaron's Antiques: Collectibles for the Discriminating Collector* in a tiny town two counties away. Squeezed between a second-hand clothing store and a long-closed bakery, the small antique shop was in an old run-down building on a narrow back street. The shop had seen more than a few hard years since it turned a profit for its owner. The building desperately needed paint, and it had apparently been months, if not years, since the shop's large window had a thorough cleaning.

Several months earlier, Margery had picked the town clean, but she had somehow failed to spot the hand-painted sign posted along the country road that also served as the town's main street. The small sign simply held the single word 'Antiques' next to a crooked arrow pointing first around the corner and then bending again towards the little shop on the narrow side street. Margery nearly missed the sign as she drove by, but it somehow seemed to call to her. She quickly turned her car around and followed the sign's directions.

Stopping in front of the antique shop, Margery examined it with the discerning eye of an experienced collector. Whereas most people would have found the shop distinctly uninviting, she deduced that its owner had fallen upon hard times, and that meant the prices should be exceptionally low.

Margery walked up to the window and peered in. The broad shelf behind the glass held the usual items: a stereopticon with a small box of paired photographs, a few tattered bibles and old books of little value, and a larger box filled with worn-out kitchen and farm tools that had long outlived their usefulness. But in one corner, something caught her eye. She walked over, but the window was so dirty, the sky so gray, and the inside of the store so poorly lit that she could only tell that it was a miniature ceramic building. Unable to wait until entering the shop, she took a tissue from her purse, spat on it, and rubbed a small clean spot on the outside of the window. Peering in, she could see it clearly.

It was a small porcelain replica of the antique shop, realistic right down to its shabby exterior with the sign *Aaron's Antiques: Collectibles for the Discriminating Collector* written in faded black letters. There was even a tiny ceramic woman looking at a collection of minuscule antiques just outside the rectangular opening representing the little shop's front window.

Margery could hardly believe her eyes. It was a single one-of-a-kind find, made directly for the store's owner. Almost all the pieces in her collection had 'Made in China' stamped across the bottom. Although a few were made long ago in an America that still manufactured such collectibles, all of her pieces came from large production runs, often numbering in the tens and sometimes even hundreds of thousands. Margery had never dared dream of owning something truly unique. Standing there on the sidewalk, she resolved to buy it, no matter the cost.

Margery opened the front door, which hit a bell that jingled loudly as she entered the quiet shop. Like the storefront, the shop's insides were dingy. Cobwebs and a fine layer of dust lay on the items displayed for the infrequent customer.

A minute later, a second door in the back opened, and an elderly man stooped with age slowly stepped into the room. The shopkeeper stopped and carefully closed the door behind him before turning and walking up to where an antique cash register stood on the counter.

"Can I help you find something, ma'am?" he asked with a voice as old and dry as the dust that covered every surface in the room.

As her eyes adjusted to the dim light from the dingy window, Margery could see that the owner was an antique himself. *He must be over 90,* she thought as she stared at the many wrinkles engraved into the leathery skin of his face and hands. Not wishing to reveal the depth of her desire for the ceramic treasure in the shop window, she glanced around the room at the store's pitifully small selection of antiques. But she could not keep herself from glancing back at the window.

"Maybe you saw something you wish in the window?" the shopkeeper asked, having noticed the momentary movement of her eyes. "Maybe the stereopticon? There is still something quite magical about how one's eyes transform two pictures into a single image."

Margery gave her head the smallest of shakes.

"Then perhaps a book?" the old man suggested. "There are words written long ago that still have the power to enchant the reader and draw her into a long-forgotten world if only she will read them."

Again, Margery shook her head.

"Might it be a tool, then?" he offered. "Possibly a wooden rolling pin? Doing something the old way can bring one such satisfaction. A frozen pie from the store will never taste as good as one that is made by hand. Or perhaps a carpenter's mallet and chisel? Joy can be found in a finely carved piece of wood."

The shopkeeper stared deep into her eyes, and Margery felt sure he knew what she really desired. He was just toying with her. The old man knew she wasn't interested in the common junk in the window. He knew…

"Surely there is something you would like." The faintest of smiles flickered on his ancient face. He waited like some primordial reptile, his dark eyes never blinking, never turning from hers.

"The ceramic building," she finally whispered once she managed to tear her eyes from the grip of his gaze. Her reply seemed unnaturally loud in the tomb-like silence of the shop. "How much?"

Once more, an almost imperceptible smile fluttered across the old man's face. "I'm afraid it's not for sale. I made it many years ago when I opened the shop. I'm sure you understand." Again, the briefest of smiles.

"Are you certain?" Margery asked, a hint of pleading in her voice. "Surely, we could come to some sort of agreement."

The old man stood there, silently watching her, as though he were deaf to her desire.

"I could pay in cash if you don't take credit cards," Margery continued. "More than it's worth."

A part of her brain was shocked at what she was saying. Ordinarily, she would never give the owner the smallest sign of how much she might want something for fear of losing any chance of talking down the price. But she was unable to help herself. The miniature ceramic shop called to her, and she had to have it.

"I'm sorry, Ma'am. I am quite certain; the item is not for sale at any price."

Somehow, without being aware of how she got there, Margery found herself sitting behind the wheel of her car. She started the engine and was soon headed back down the country road for home and her waiting collection. But Margery had barely driven ten miles before she turned around. She had to go back. She had to convince the old man to part with his little ceramic shop. She had to. She just had to…

Once again, she pulled up in front of the antique store. She stepped out of her car and walked up to the door, prepared to argue, to confess her desire, her strange new need, and offer the old man whatever it took. But the small sign in the door window said 'Closed.'

It was growing dark, a breeze had begun to blow, and she felt the first tiny droplets of winter rain falling faintly on her face from the low gray clouds above. She glanced around, looking for anyone who might tell her where the old man lived, but the street was deserted, and the lights were out in every building. She looked down and pressed a button on the new watch her son gave her for her birthday.

The Collector

Seven PM, Sunday, the 30th of October, the green characters glowed up at her. The old man would not return until Monday morning. The rain was pouring in earnest now. The clouds were racing overhead, and the cold wind cut through her light coat. Soon, she would be drenched to the bone.

Margery turned around, intending to get back into her car, but then she saw it. Lying on the ground was a brick. She looked around, but there were no other bricks nearby. It was almost as though it had been left there for her. As if in a dream, she bent down and picked it up. She felt its rough, heavy weight in her hand, cold and wet. Just an ordinary brick…

Perhaps it was the frustration. Maybe it was anger at the old man for refusing to sell to her. Perhaps it was a feeling for which she had no name. Whatever it was, she spun around without thinking and flung the brick with all her might at the antique shop's window. She was startled by the incredible loudness of the breaking glass. She stood still for an instant, shocked at what she had done. Then, looking around to make sure she was alone, she walked up to the window and reached in…

…

The next morning, the old shopkeeper slowly walked up to his store, just as he had each morning for sixty years. The store window, as always, remained dingy but not so much that customers couldn't see the items inside. He bent over and peered through the small circle of glass Margery had cleaned the previous day. The small ceramic shop sat there as it had the day before, but with one exception. The tiny female figurine was no longer standing in front of the little shop's window. Instead, it was standing inside.

The old man smiled as he unlocked the door to his antique store and stepped inside. He walked over to the small ceramic copy of his shop and carefully carried it into his private office. Opening the back of the little building, he reached in and gently removed the tiny ceramic statuette. He sat down at his desk and admired her under his large, lighted magnifying glass. She was exquisite, perfect in every detail, from the pink polish on her tiny porcelain fingernails to her wide-eyed expression of shocked surprise.

With loving tenderness, the shopkeeper carefully carried her over to his curio cabinet. He placed her inside with the dozens of other tiny statuettes in his collection, setting her between a Civil War soldier and a slender young woman in a beaded flapper dress. The figurines silently watched the old man, their eyes following him as he locked the cabinet door and slowly shuffled back to his desk.

"Perhaps a man this time," the shopkeeper whispered to himself as he turned back to the small ceramic copy of his shop. "Maybe a man in a leather jacket looking for a gift for his girlfriend."

He reached into a desk drawer and pulled out a crude ceramic figurine of a man. Picking up his miniature shop and the tiny male statuette, the old man carried them to their special place inside the storefront window. Then, he returned to his office to admire his collection while he patiently waited for his next collectible.

Author's Comments

The idea for this story came one night as I was trying to fall asleep. My wife collects Christmas towns, and I collect old books and oddities that properly belong in a curio cabinet. If collectors collect collectibles, then who collects collectors?

GRANDMA BUFORD'S BIRTHDAY

Miss Beulah May Buford, of the Charleston Bufords, had been looking forward to this day for several months. It was her birthday, her 97th birthday, and she eagerly anticipated the arrival of four generations of Bufords who would gather around her in the day room of the Shady Grove Nursing Home. It was a family tradition for the entire Buford clan to come together and celebrate their matriarch's birthday.

Although Miss Buford did not approve of everyone who had married into the Buford clan, she would never dream of letting the lamentable choices of some of her many descendants put a damper on her day. Not if she could enjoy the new babies and gush over how much the toddlers had grown. The children all called her grandma, a title Miss Buford thought far superior to that of mother, now that she was no longer responsible for the hard work of raising children.

So far, she had endured the indignity of having one of the nurses bathe her and help her into the white dress she wore just once a year on her birthday. *How did I lose so much weight?* Miss Buford thought when she realized that the dress sorely needed to be taken in a size or two. *I really must eat more than one piece of cake, even if it means I'll pay for it later.* No bout of bellyache was going to keep the old woman from enjoying her special day.

Miss Buford didn't move a muscle as she patiently waited for her beautician to finish brushing

Grandma Buford's Birthday

her wig and apply her makeup. Although the young woman used altogether too much powder on her sunken cheeks, the Buford matriarch wasn't about to complain. Sadly, the increasingly annoying tremors of her age-spotted hands had made "putting on her Sunday face," as she liked to call her morning ritual, impossible.

They'll be here soon, Miss Buford silently thought as the woman put on the finishing touches to her makeup. *What's taking that girl so long?* She would have said something to her about it, but the young woman wore a pair of earbuds and was listening to music that would surely drown out Miss Buford's voice, which had grown progressively weaker over the preceding months.

The beautician finished and stepped back to admire her handiwork. "There, that's better," she observed. "You look good, even if I do say so myself."

Finally, all her preparations were completed. Miss Buford was rolled out to the common room, where she had nothing to do but wait for the many members of her clan to come and gather around their aged matriarch. And arrive they did. What's more, several of her oldest and closest friends had also arrived to help her celebrate. Soon, they would step forward, give her their gifts, and help her open them. She would smile and invite the children up to wish her a happy birthday and kiss her papery cheek.

Someone started playing the organ that sat in a corner by the window, and the first of many stepped forward. "Happy birthday, Grandma Buford," a woman in her thirties said. *I think that must be Ida, my great, great niece on Herbert's side,* the old woman thought. *Or is it Jackson's wife, Suzanne? There are so many to keep track of, and my memory isn't what it once was.*

Grandma Buford's cataracts had slowly worsened until everything had taken on a misty gray as though she were in a dense fog. *And neither are my eyes,* she thought. *It's so hard to see anymore. I wish the woman would come closer.*

A young girl of eight or nine stood next to her mother. Ida nodded encouragingly and placed a hand on her daughter's shoulders. "It's okay, Mary," she said.

The young girl hesitated and then reluctantly moved forward. She bent down to kiss her grandmother's cheek. But at the last second, she pulled back and turned to her mother. "I'm sorry, momma. I can't. I know it's a family tradition, but I just can't. Besides, that's not Grandma, not really."

Miss Buford didn't know what to think. *Why, I'm here, child. Right here.*

"That's okay, Mary. You're right. She's in a better place now. She's with the Lord, and he's taken away all her earthly pain. Her suffering is over and gone forever."

Miss Buford was positively perplexed, but as she drifted away, she realized the truth. *Oh, my... This isn't really a birthday party, and I'm not at Shady Grove after all; I'm at a funeral home... I'm coming, Grandpa. I'm finally coming home...*

Author's Comments

This short story actually came to me in a dream, in which I was surprised to find myself being prepared for my own funeral.

THE FARMER'S DAUGHTER

It was the day before Thanksgiving, and I had been driving since well before dawn. The only time I stopped was to buy gas or to go through the drive-through at some fast-food restaurant along the way. But most of the time, I just ate in my car while driving. It was an eighteen-hour drive from the University of New Mexico to my parent's place in Minneapolis. I had no time to spare if I wanted to get home in time for my family's holiday feast. Although I really loved the freedom that came with being away at college, I was more homesick than I would ever admit to my friends. That, and I was eagerly looking forward to my mom's cooking after eating three meals a day at the campus cafeteria since the start of the school year.

And so, the day passed slowly as I drove my battered old car across New Mexico, bits of Texas and Oklahoma, and Kansas. I had just passed the Missouri state line when the first fat flakes of snow began to fall. It was snowing heavily by the time I crossed into Iowa, and the tiny flakes finally forced me to face reality. My plans for driving all the way home without stopping had been wildly over-optimistic. Trying to make up time, I left my original highway and drove cross-country on a road that took me almost directly home. But my plans quickly proved disastrous. Had I been listening to the local radio stations, I would have learned that the first big snowstorm of the season was barreling toward me.

The Farmer's Daughter

Only a few minutes earlier, the snow had just been gently drifting down. But now, it was blowing sideways and so thick that my car's headlights merely made it harder to see. The balding tires on my old car began losing their grip on the icy road, and it didn't help that I was getting sleepy and having trouble staying awake.

The inevitable happened.

My eyes closed briefly, and by the time I reopened them, my car was already drifting off the road. Before I could react, I was in some farmer's field with barbed wire wrapped around the front of my car. Angrily placing it in reverse, I tried to back up onto the road, but the tires just spun on the icy ground. I was stuck.

Except for my headlights reflecting off trillions of falling snowflakes, it was totally dark. It was then that I realized that I hadn't passed a farmhouse or car for at least an hour, not since I'd left the freeway for the isolation of that straight backcountry road. I began to worry. With my gas gauge nearly on empty, I was bound to run out of gas before dawn if I kept the engine running. But if I didn't, I could well freeze to death. Because I knew that I'd have everything I needed once I reached home, I hardly brought anything with me. More importantly, I didn't have any blankets or heavy winter clothes to wrap up in.

I didn't have much hope when I turned off the headlights to see any nearby farmhouse or perhaps the light from some small town reflecting off the low clouds overhead. But all I saw was darkness, and all I heard was the sound of the snow beating against the car's windows. I had no choice but to leave the engine running, the heater on, and to try to wait out the night. I wrapped my thin jacket tightly around me, leaned back, and eventually drifted off into a deep, dreamless sleep.

Something woke me up. At first, I wasn't sure what it was, but the silence and cold soon made it clear. The engine had stopped running. I tried starting it again, but it just turned over without catching. I turned on the dash lights; the gas gauge read empty. Turning off the lights, I sat in the darkness, disgusted at myself for not stopping sooner to refill the tank. Then, something, I don't know what, seemed to call to me, prompting me to look once more into the darkness and the falling snow.

Far off, at the edge of sight, I saw a pale, cold light that flickered briefly, half-hidden behind the falling snow. It disappeared. Desperately, I used the sleeve of my jacket to rub my side window free from the frost forming on it. And then, I saw it again, brighter this time as if the curtain of snow had briefly parted in the freezing air between us.

Desperate times called for drastic measures. Although I had heard many times that it was safer to stay in your car when stuck in the snow, I also knew that no one knew where I was and that the road I was on was little traveled. So, I decided to abandon my car and place my fate in that flickering light in the night.

The Farmer's Daughter

I opened the door, and the cold air nearly drove me back inside. Then, steeling my courage, I ignored the icy bite of the tiny flakes on my bare skin and headed out into the darkness.

After a hundred yards or so, I could see the source of the light. It was a large old farmhouse, set well back from the road between two giant oak trees, the only trees I'd seen for miles in that flat Iowa countryside. The light was a large candle burning in a downstairs window. I would never have seen it were it not for the lack of all other sources of light. I walked as fast as I could, with the cold cutting through my jacket and biting into my bones.

Finally, I reached the house and trudged up the steps onto its covered porch. I stomped my feet to remove some of the snow that had caked onto my socks and knocked on the door.

Nothing happened.

I pounded again, as hard as my freezing hands would permit, but once more, the only answer was the loud booming of my knocking reverberating through the darkened house.

Then I saw a flickering light approach through the door's stained-glass window, and it opened.

A beautiful young girl, nearly my own age, stood in the darkened doorway. She held an oil lamp in one hand and used the other to wrap her thin robe tightly around her slender body. But instead of looking at me, she gazed out over my shoulder, staring into the night as if she had been anxiously waiting for someone else. Then with her hopes dashed, she hung her head with disappointment and gestured for me to follow her inside.

I was shivering so hard from the cold that I barely managed to say "Thank you" as I joined her in the darkened entryway of the empty house. Then I noticed that I could see my breath in the pale light of her lamp. The house seemed little warmer than outside, though I was happy to be out of the wind and snow.

The girl then turned and stared into my face as if truly noticing me for the first time. With a look of concern, she had me follow her into the parlor. After sitting me down in a big leather chair and wrapping a comforter around my shoulders, she bent down to add some wood to the remaining coals that glowed amid the ashes of the fireplace. Then, without a word, she walked silently out of the room before I could introduce myself or tell her what had happened. As the wood caught fire, and the flames began to light the dark recesses of the room, I could hear her moving about in the kitchen and the sound of a pan being placed on the stove.

The fire began to give off the most wonderful warmth as it crackled and hissed. I leaned forward to rub my icy fingers in front of the flames.

A few minutes later, she returned, carrying a large mug full of hot apple cider that she carefully placed in my hands. Wrapping my still frigid fingers around the cup, I took a sip of the steaming cider, smiled, and then drank all of it.

I thanked her again, gratefully smiling up at her. I told her that I had been on my way home from school and dozed off while driving. I explained that I'd run my car into the field just down the road, and now it was stuck in the snow. I asked to use her phone, so I could call my parents. I wanted to let them know I was all right but wouldn't be home tonight as I'd planned.

She nodded and led me into the hallway, where she pointed to an old antique phone mounted on the wall. I lifted the receiver and was about to dial when I realized that there was no dial tone.

I told her that the phone was out and asked her if she had a cell phone I could use. But she just looked at me with a funny expression on her face and shook her head.

Realizing that I hadn't introduced myself, I told her my name. She said hers was Crystal and that her parents were away visiting her sick grandmother in Topeka. They weren't due back until the next afternoon for the family Thanksgiving dinner.

After an awkward pause, Crystal led me back to the parlor, and we sat down in front of the fireplace. Almost instantly, I was nodding off, and I must have fallen asleep because the next thing I remember, I felt her hand on my shoulder gently waking me. She led me upstairs to a spare bedroom, and I was asleep in seconds.

The next day, I was awakened by the sound of her calling my name. Brilliant sunlight streamed in through the window. On rising, I could see that the surrounding fields were covered in a beautiful bright blanket of fresh snow and that the road was blocked by drifts, some of which were a couple of feet high.

It was clear I was going nowhere until it melted. As I stepped out into the hallway, the wonderful smell of frying eggs and ham drifted up from the kitchen. I walked in just as she was getting ready to dish up our breakfasts.

Crystal told me about growing up on the farm, graduating from the local high school, and how totally quiet the house had been since her parents had left the previous week. She asked me about what my college was like and the classes I was taking. And I also told her of my childhood and my family, and even my ambitions and dreams once I graduated.

It was a perfect meal. I'd never felt so comfortable with anyone in my life. Crystal listened intently to everything I said as if hungry for the mere sound of my voice, as if she hadn't talked to anyone for ages. And I found her rapt attention amazingly attractive and her intent gaze seductive. And she was stunningly beautiful with long straight black hair and the pale skin of someone who never spent time outside under the sun.

After such a great breakfast, I helped Crystal clear the table and wash the dishes. Somehow, doing them by hand wasn't really work when I had her by my side. We spent the rest of the morning playing games: dominos, checkers, cards, and even chess. I hardly cared when I discovered that the electricity was out and there was no television.

Later, after an excellent lunch, Crystal started getting food out and asked me to help her fix the Thanksgiving dinner. She started cooking a large turkey in the gas oven, and I was soon busy peeling potatoes, opening jars of home-canned vegetables, and learning how to bake bread and pies from scratch.

Crystal and I worked and talked all afternoon. Time just seemed to fly, and soon we were making salads and setting the table. The turkey and home-baked bread smelled fantastic, the mashed potatoes and bowls of green beans and corn were ready, and all we needed was for her parents to arrive. Every so often, we would go to the windows and look out at the road. However, we never saw anything, not even the tracks of cars that might have passed while we had been busy fixing dinner. Though the snowdrifts weren't huge, they were still big enough to block the road.

And so, we waited and waited as it grew dark, and evening came. And still, we waited as the candles on the table slowly burned down in their holders. The mashed potatoes had long been cold, the bread was getting hard, and the turkey was drying out, and still, we waited. Crystal became more and more nervous and upset as her parents failed to arrive. Eventually, when it became clear they wouldn't make it until the next day, I suggested we sit down and celebrate Thanksgiving together. I'm sure it would have been better had we started eating when the meal was warm from the stove, but I don't think it really mattered. It was still a wonderful, old-fashioned dinner, and we ate it together. I was happy to just talk with her, and once she had resigned herself to waiting another day, it wasn't long before she was smiling again.

After we'd stuffed ourselves, we got up, leaving the table and dirty dishes for the morning. We returned to the parlor, I built another fire, and Crystal played the piano for me. They were quaint old songs that I remember my grandmother listening to on her old wind-up Victrola. Somehow, they just seemed to fit the old farmhouse and the traditional meal we'd just finished. Then, she went back into the kitchen, brought out a couple of slices of apple pie, and we sat down on the couch and watched the flames from the fire flicker and fly up the chimney. It was truly magical, and I wanted nothing more than for the evening to never end.

But eventually, it did. As it neared midnight, Crystal said she was sleepy, and we stood up and headed for the stairs. She saw me to my room, gave me a warm kiss goodnight, and then headed down the hall to her room. I sat down on the bed and realized that I was in love with her. I went to sleep wondering how we could spend more time together and decided that I would rather spend Christmas break in this old Iowa farmhouse than with my family in Minneapolis.

The next day, I slept in until mid-morning. On finally waking up, I rose and looked at my reflection in the big mirror on the dresser. I was smiling ear to ear as my memories of the day before came back to me. I even began to whistle as I glanced out the window of my room to a clear blue sky and brilliant sunlight shining down on the farmer's fields. The weather had warmed up, and the snow was rapidly melting so that there were bare spots on the road. It

The Farmer's Daughter

looked like I'd be able to get my car out of the field if I could just borrow some gas.

I went downstairs, but Crystal wasn't in the kitchen, fixing breakfast as she had been the day before. I called out her name, thinking that she was just in some other part of the house, but all I heard was silence. I quickly checked every room but didn't find her. I began to worry that something terrible might have happened. I even went up into the attic and checked down into the basement. But still no Crystal.

Then thinking that I'd find her outside, I went out and looked in the barn and shed, but all I found was a can of gasoline. I carried it out to my car and poured it into the empty gas tank. Then, getting in, I turned the key, and the engine started right up. Although the wheels spun a little in the wet ground, I managed to back my car out onto the road on the third try and drive back to the house. I opened the door and called her. But again, there was no answer.

I was about to look for her again, but then I remembered that I hadn't called my parents the previous night. I checked the phone, but it was still out. So, thinking that she must have just gone for a walk in the fields, I wrote Crystal a note saying that I'd be back as soon as I had driven into town to call my folks.

About ten miles down the road, I came to a small Iowa farm town dominated by a couple of grain elevators. The road became Main Street with a few stores, a church, and a single gas station. I parked in front of the town's lone diner and went in.

A Cauldron of Uncanny Dreams

Despite the previous day's huge Thanksgiving dinner, I suddenly realized I was ravenous as if I hadn't eaten for days. I wolfed down a large stack of pancakes and then headed to the pay phone in the back next to a counter at which an old man in his seventies sat in faded overalls, nursing his cup of coffee.

I called home, and my mom answered immediately. She said she'd been worried when she heard about the terrible storm on the news. She had been especially anxious when I hadn't called in from some motel along the way. I reassured her, telling her where I was, that I was fine, and that I would head home again later that afternoon. She asked me why I wasn't heading home right then, given that I had already lost a day because of the storm, and so I told her about getting stuck, finding Crystal's farm, and staying two nights there with her. From what she said and how she said it, I could tell she was both grateful that I'd found a place to stay but also concerned about me staying in some strange woman's home. So I tried to reassure her by describing Crystal, what we had done on Thanksgiving, and the farm she lived on. I explained that was why I wouldn't be heading right back; I wanted to thank her and say goodbye properly. I didn't tell her that I also wanted to set up a way for Crystal and me to keep in touch and hopefully spend part of Christmas break with her. Then I told my mom goodbye and turned to go.

The old man was staring at me with the weirdest expression. It was as if he couldn't tell whether he'd

The Farmer's Daughter

seen a ghost or if I was somehow completely crazy. I was about to walk past him when he grabbed my arm with unexpected strength and demanded to know where I'd spent the night. I told him that it was none of his business, but if he had to know, I'd stayed at a big old farmhouse between two giant oak trees about ten miles down the road. Then, becoming deathly white, he demanded to know who lived there. I had barely said Crystal's name when he jumped up and ran out of the restaurant, nearly knocking the waitress over in the process.

I stared at him through the diner's front window as he roared out of his parking place and then turned to the waitress who now stood behind the counter. I asked her what was with the old man. She told me not to mind him. She said that he'd never been quite right for the last thirty years, not since he and his wife had come back from a trip the day after Thanksgiving to learn that his house had burned down the previous night. He'd lost his daughter in the fire and his wife had died just a few years later. He'd been broken and lost ever since.

It was a sad story, but I didn't really give it much thought. I was eager to get back to Crystal and spend a few more hours with her before I had to continue on towards home. After stopping briefly to fill up the gas tank, I drove back through the small town and headed west towards the farmhouse and the girl who'd suddenly become such an important part of my life. Although I'd only been gone for about an hour, I already missed her and was angry with myself for not looking harder for her before I left. I was also upset that I hadn't had a chance to say goodbye and hoped that she'd seen my note and understood why I'd driven into town without finding her first. I didn't want her to think I'd left without even a goodbye. Maybe it was just that I'd been unnerved by the crazy old man. I drove the memory of him from my mind and thought only of her beauty and tenderness and our first kiss the night before.

It wasn't long before I saw the farm's two tall trees on the horizon. But even from that distance, something seemed strange. When I drew closer, I understood. I'd just been mistaken because no old farmhouse stood between them. I thought it odd that I hadn't remembered passing them on my way into town, but I was probably just in a hurry to get there, call home, fill up the tank, and return.

Getting closer, I saw an old car parked along the side of the road. I was slowing down to pass it when I noticed the broken chimney and ancient ruins of a fire on the foundation where an old farmhouse once stood. Glancing over at the car, I saw the old man from the diner sitting slumped behind the wheel. No wonder, I thought, given the similar trees and the burned-down farmhouse. No wonder the old man had been confused when he'd overheard me describing the place to my parents over the phone. The resemblance was striking. Yet, surely most old farmhouses had big trees in their yards. I'd just have to drive farther down the road until I found the right one where Crystal surely waited for me.

The Farmer's Daughter

And then I saw the hole in the barbwire fence and the fresh ruts that my tires had left on the snowy ground. My blood froze as my car skidded to a stop.

With a deepening sense of dread, I got out and looked down at the footprints my shoes had left in the snow that morning. I staggered back to where the old man sat in his car. He opened his door, stepped out, and stood sadly waiting for me.

As I joined the old man to stare at the ruin of his home, he asked me if this was the place where I'd spent Thanksgiving. I answered that it couldn't be. I'd just left the house an hour ago, and everything was fine. There had to be some mistake. Again, he asked me what the girl's name was, and I told him. He nodded knowingly and then sadly told me how he and his wife had gone to visit her sick mother in Topeka. He told me how their daughter, Crystal, had decided to stay behind to cook the traditional Thanksgiving feast. He told me how they had not made it home in time to share the meal with her because they'd been stuck in a giant snowstorm and couldn't get through. And finally, he told me how they had returned the following day to the still-smoking ruins of his farmhouse. There had been a terrible fire, and the volunteer fire chief had said that Crystal had died in the blaze.

But my mind rebelled; I couldn't believe that it was the same place. There had to be another farmhouse just down the road. Wasn't there another family with a girl named Crystal that lived nearby? Surely, we weren't talking about the same Crystal.

But he told me that there wasn't another farmhouse for miles and that this was the only place with two tall trees in the yard. He said that Crystal had promised that she'd have Thanksgiving dinner ready for them when they got home. All these years, her spirit was trapped between this world and the next, waiting for some way to fulfill her promise. And then I came. Maybe it was something about the snowstorm. Perhaps it was the danger I had been in. But whatever it was, I had finally let her keep her promise, and for that, he was grateful. Maybe now she could finally rest in peace.

I didn't want to listen to him, and I certainly didn't want to believe him. I ran back to my car and drove off. I must have spent the entire day driving up and down the roads outside of that small Iowa town, but I never did find the farm. I was finally forced to accept that the old man was right. I'm not sure whether Crystal was a ghost haunting a ghostly farmhouse or whether the storm had somehow transported me back in time to that fateful Thanksgiving just before she had died. Either way, it didn't matter. I would never see her again. But wherever she is, I hope she remembers me. I know I will never forget her.

Author's Comments

This is the oldest story in the anthology. While reading a book of fairy tales some thirty years ago, I came across the story of a roving knight who happened upon an isolated castle. He spent the night

The Farmer's Daughter

as an honored guest, only to wake up the next morning in the ruins of a long-fallen fortress.

THE HAUNTING OF THE EDERESCU HOUSE

My name is Jacob McKinzie. I'm a paranormal investigator, and I write books about haunted buildings. To pay the bills and finance my investigations, I also work as a staff researcher for the TV series, *Is Your House Haunted?* I'm one of the people who finds houses that would make good episodes for the show. This is the story of a house that nearly made the cut, that would have made a hell of an episode if unforeseen circumstances hadn't intervened.

It was ten minutes until midnight on a cold October evening when I arrived in the tiny town of Bogdan, Indiana. Little more than a wide spot in the road, Bogdan is just a score of small businesses — several of which were boarded up — and a few dozen run-down houses arranged on either side of the county road that forms the tiny town's main street. I learned on the Internet that Romanian emigrants founded Bogdan in the late 1800s. According to Wikipedia, the otherwise obscure little town's main claim to fame is its Founders Day celebration, when the small population dresses up in traditional garb, eats traditional Romanian dishes, and performs traditional dances to traditional folksongs. In other words, for one day out of the year, Bogdan transports itself back through time

The Haunting of the Ederescu House

to a Romania that hasn't existed for well over a hundred years.

After checking into the town's only motel and unpacking my clothes and equipment, I took out my laptop and once more went over what little I had been able to glean about the house I had come to see. I'm not sure why I chose the Ederescu house. There are undoubtedly many haunted buildings that are much more infamous. In fact, there was damned little that I'd been able to learn from my Internet search. I couldn't even remember when or from whom I had heard about it. All I knew was that there had been a particularly gruesome murder-suicide. Shortly after that, an article in the local, now-defunct newspaper mentioned rumors of a haunting. Yet despite the lack of information, there was something about the newspaper's photo of the abandoned house that whispered to me, *Come. Come to me. Come to me now!*

According to the article, a man named Omor Ederescu had beaten his wife and son to death in a drunken rage. The next morning, someone had found their badly beaten bodies in the family's kitchen. Omor's body, however, was found in the basement where he had hung himself, a knocked-over chair lying just out of reach at his feet. Omor's brother then inherited the house, and both he and his wife were found murdered in bed several weeks after moving in. Upon the brother's death, his eldest son inherited the house but only lived in it a few days before moving out. The house has remained empty ever since, abandoned by its owner and left to slowly decay. Rumors of a ghost have grown over the subsequent fifty years, and few now dared enter the Ederescu house.

The following day dawned cold and damp with a solid ceiling of dreary gray clouds covering the sky. Although the weather forecast called for afternoon rains, a steady drizzle had already begun.

After breakfast in the Dunarea Diner, Bogdan's only restaurant, I began my investigation by driving out to the house. Several miles west of the small town, it stood by itself some thirty yards back from the road. I pulled into the driveway, stepped out of my car, and took a few photographs of the dilapidated two-story farmhouse.

At first glance, the Ederescu house was just what one would expect after being abandoned for five decades. Large patches of paint had peeled off its weathered clapboard siding, and its windows had all been broken — no doubt by kids throwing rocks.

The only uncanny aspect of the house was its yard. The two trees in the front were dead, standing like giant scarecrows with their smaller branches lying broken and rotting on the ground. Their bark had long ago sloughed off, leaving large patches of mold and fungus covering the leprous wood. Nothing grew within five feet of the house, no overgrown bushes or weeds, not even a single blade of grass. It was as though someone had covered the ground in salt to imprison some nameless evil inside. Farther away, a few dead and dying weeds rose like wounded soldiers, barely remaining upright over the bodies of their fallen brethren. Compared to the

The Haunting of the Ederescu House

yard, the weeds in the ditch across the road from the farm were green and lush.

Before actually entering the Ederescu house, I wanted to learn more about it and its history. Because the local newspaper had gone out of business some years earlier, I asked the men I found at the town barbershop. They told me to talk to Grigore Luka, who acted as the town's unofficial historian. I followed their directions to a modest home down a narrow side street and knocked on the door. The elderly gentleman with thinning gray hair that answered the door gave me a look of mingled curiosity and suspicion. After introducing myself, explaining my purpose, and clarifying that I wasn't a salesman, Mr. Luka invited me in. It turned out that the old man lived alone, his wife having died several years ago. He was only too happy to share his extensive knowledge of the town with a complete stranger.

After making us tea, Mr. Luka sat down opposite me in his threadbare armchair and began to speak. At the time of the murders, Omor Ederescu was well on his way to becoming the town drunk. Worse, he was an angry drunk whose cruelty and rage were set free in direct proportion to the amount of alcohol he had consumed. Mean-spirited and belligerent, he was a man who was mad at the entire world. An irreligious man in a town centered on its single Romanian orthodox church, he would loudly curse the mayor, the shopkeepers, the priest, and the farmhands who worked his fields. He especially cursed his wife, Izabela, both loudly and often, for nagging him about his drinking. Regularly, people would see her coming into town with bruises on her face and arms, and her excuses of having "accidents" fooled no one.

Although there were no witnesses to the horrible crime, it was clear to the entire town what had happened. Late one Saturday evening after staggering home from the town's bar, Omor once more began beating his wife. However, this time was different from so many times before. His son, Vilhelm, was no longer a mere child but fourteen years old and becoming a young man. Vilhelm tried to protect his mother, but this "betrayal" of his father had only further enraged Omor, who beat his son to death and strangled his wife. After drinking every bottle in the house dry, Omor passed out and didn't wake until midday. On discovering the bodies in the kitchen, Omor remembered what he had done. He descended into the basement, tied a noose to an overhead water pipe, and hung himself.

Noticing that neither Omor's wife nor son attended the Sunday mass, the priest grew concerned and drove out to the Ederescu's farm. There, he found the cold dead bodies of Izabela and Vilhelm lying on the kitchen floor amid shattered dishes, overturned chairs, and several broken vodka bottles. Searching the rest of the house, the priest found Omor's lifeless body in the basement. Unlike his wife and son, the father's body was still warm. He had hung himself less than an hour before the priest had arrived.

The Haunting of the Ederescu House

The murder-suicide was a great scandal in the town. Every man, woman, and child was horrified by the tragedy and mourned the violent deaths of Omor's poor wife and son. But no one mourned for Omor, and many said that he would not escape his punishment in Hell even if his suicide had prevented punishment by the law.

For three days, Izabela and Vilhelm's coffins rested on tables in the living room of the Ederescu house as mourners paid their respects. Mirrors were draped in black cloth so that their spirits would not wander into them and be trapped. Candles remained lit, and the mourners placed coins in the hands of both mother and son so they could pay the toll on their way to the afterlife. More importantly, Omor's brother, Stefan, performed the night watch. By standing guard over the bodies of his sister-in-law and nephew, he protected their bodies from evil spirits that could enter their remains, enabling them to return to haunt the living. Afterward, they were given a traditional Romanian Orthodox funeral service and buried in the town cemetery.

Omor, on the other hand, received no such wake or funeral service, and no one performed the night watch over his body. Instead, his corpse was dumped unceremoniously into an unmarked grave in the field behind the house. And because he had lived a life of sin and died by suicide, Omor was buried facedown with cloves of garlic under his tongue to prevent him from returning as a strigoi — an undead corpse that walked the night to hunt the living.

A Cauldron of Uncanny Dreams

After the funeral, Omor's brother, Stefan, inherited the Ederescu farm. Being a pious couple who placed their faith in God, Stefan and his wife, Crina, were unafraid and moved into the farmhouse where his brother's family had died. Soon afterward, Stefan noticed that a previously full bottle of vodka was nearly empty the following morning. He found this exceedingly strange as Crina did not drink, and they were the only ones in the house. Things became more serious when Crina began to wake up with mysterious bruises on her face and arms. Rumors began to spread that Stefan, like his brother Omor, beat his wife, but the pair vigorously denied it. Over the following days, her bruises became more common and more noticeable.

Finally, one night, Stefan was awakened by the moans of his sleeping wife. Turning over to wake her from her nightmare, Stefan saw the silhouette of a stranger standing by the bed and leaning over his wife! Clouds that had hidden the full moon parted, and Stefan recognized the face of his dead brother in the dim light shining in through the window. Terrified, Stefan shouted out his brother's name, waking his wife from her nightmare. Jumping out of bed, he turned to confront the apparition, but it was gone, and his wife had fresh bruises on her face and arms.

The rest of the night, Stefan stayed up and watched over his sleeping wife. The next morning, he discovered his vodka bottle lying empty on the kitchen floor. Stefan told Vasile, his grown son, who lived in town, what happened, and the two of them agreed that there could only be one explanation.

Being a sinful man who died by suicide, an evil spirit entered Omor's corpse, turning it into a strigoi. This enabled the undead monster to leave its grave and haunt the living. So, Stefan and Vasile did what had to be done. They dug up the rotting corpse and pounded a stake through its heart, nailing it to the ground so it could never rise again.

At first, their desperate deed seemed to have succeeded, but their success was short-lived. The following Sunday morning, Stefan and Crina also failed to attend mass. After the service, Vasile and the priest traveled to the Ederescu farm. There, they found the kitchen chairs knocked over, small items scattered about, and an empty vodka bottle smashed on the floor. Much worse, they found the bodies of Stefan and Crina lying dead in their bed. She had terrible bruises over her entire body, while her husband had a single bruise that circled his neck, the same type of bruise that the rope had given Omor. For the second time in a month, the town attended a wake, and the priest performed the funeral service. This time, it was Vasile's turn to stand night watch over his parents' bodies, and the next day, they were given a proper burial.

Vasile inherited the farm, and like his father before him, he planned to move into the house and work the surrounding fields. But before he did anything else, he once more dug up his uncle's unmarked grave. This time, Vasile cut off the corpse's head and burned it in a large bonfire until nothing, but ashes remained. He also had the priest bless his house so that no evil would dare enter.

However, Omor's ghost would not be so easily stopped. At midnight that very night, Vasile awoke, gasping for breath with a terrible pain in his neck. There at the foot of his bed stood the headless rotting corpse of his uncle Omor. The suffocating stench of death and decay filled the room. Vasile threw back the covers and rose to confront the horrible apparition, but it had vanished, as it had with his father. Nearly strangled, Vasile's body was covered in bruises as though the ghost had almost beaten him to death. He fled the house and drove into town to await the dawn. The next morning, he again dug up Omor's rotting corpse. Because burning his uncle's head had decapitated the ghost, Vasile believed that burning the rest of Omor's remains would surely destroy the strigoi and send the demon inhabiting it back to Hell.

Despite reducing the remains to ashes, Vasile abandoned the Ederescu house and moved back to his small apartment in town. He worked the farm during the day, but every night, he returned to the safety of Bogdan. Vasile let the house fall into ruin. Eventually, when he grew old and died, the farm was sold. Like Vasile before him, the new owner lives in town and will not enter the house, neither by day nor by night. And that is how the house remains today: abandoned, feared, and shunned by the inhabitants of Bogdan.

Once the town historian had finished his tale, I thanked him and returned to my hotel room to write up what I had learned and to decide on my next steps. Mr. Luka's recollection matched what I had read in the newspaper article I had found online. Even better, filming an interview with the elderly man with his Romanian accent would make a great addition to the TV show.

After lunch, I would visit the house and take pictures to show the producers and members of the cast. After another dinner at the diner, I would return to the Ederescu house to set up my infrared and low-light cameras, recording thermometers, and other equipment. Then, I would spend the night and learn whether there was any truth to the supernatural aspects of Mr. Luka's tale.

After a quick lunch and returning to the motel to pick up my equipment, I drove out to the Ederescu farm and parked in front of the house. Not surprisingly, the front door lock had been broken, probably by teenagers entering the house on a dare.

Upon stepping into the house, the first thing I noticed was the smell. It was more than just the smell of mildew and decay. It was the musty smell I had smelled only once before... in the catacombs under Paris. It was an unexpected smell because Mr. Luka had not mentioned anyone being buried beneath the house. The second thing I noticed was the temperature. Although it was a typical dreary late October day — cold, a solid gray sky, and drizzle interrupted by showers — it seemed to be a good ten degrees colder inside than out. Of course, it might have just been my imagination; to be sure,

I'd have to measure the temperature when I set up my equipment.

Apparently, Vasile Ederescu had felt that the plain furniture he had inherited was not worth taking. The chairs and tables in the front room and dining room — which were neither new nor old enough to be antiques — were still where they had been when he abandoned the house. He had even left the oil lamps and the family photographs on the walls. The only things that didn't belong were a few empty beer cans and bottles earlier visitors had thrown into the corner. I took several photographs before moving on.

Glancing into the bathroom, I suspected the same individuals who had left the beer cans had also used the toilet after the water had been turned off. However, the bowl's contents were bone dry and so old that little stench remained.

That only left the kitchen on the ground floor. Here, the table and chairs had been broken, their pieces scattered across the floor. Smashed dishes and shattered glass littered the worn linoleum flooring while the cabinets' contents lay strewn across the kitchen counters. A broken vodka bottle lay beneath a bottle-shaped hole in the plaster wall. Everywhere, there was clear evidence of an altercation, though between who I had no idea. I opened the cabinets and found them full of dishes as well as cans and boxes of fifty-year-old food. Nothing had been touched, not even by mice, if the surprising lack of droppings was any indication. I took more photos, including several of the vodka

The Haunting of the Ederescu House

bottles that were tied to Mr. Luka's description of Omor as a violent alcoholic.

Next, I climbed the narrow stairs to the second floor with its four small bedrooms. Luckily, the roof had held up to the Indiana winters, so I didn't have to worry about falling through rain-rotted floorboards. One of the rooms, slightly larger than the rest, must have been the master bedroom where Omor's apparition had made its appearance.

The bed covers still lay where Vasile had flung them in his haste to stand and face his dead uncle. I wondered how he must have felt sleeping in the very same bed in which his parents had been so brutally murdered. Though covered with fifty years' worth of dust and the droppings of birds that had flown in through the broken windows, I could still see the remains of a set of muddy footprints. They led directly from a window at the back of the house to the foot of the bed before vanishing as eerily as they had appeared. Could they have really been the footsteps of Omor's corpse, or had someone purposely left them there as a cruel hoax? I took photos of the bed, the footprints, and through the window to the field where Omor was buried.

I had saved the best for last: the basement where Omor had hanged himself. Whereas the weak light coming through the house's broken windows provided adequate illumination to the rest of the house, the cellar had neither windows nor an outside door. I went out to my car and returned with a powerful flashlight and an electric lantern for illuminating an entire room. The stairs creaked loudly with each step that I descended into the darkness but held my weight without collapsing.

Everywhere I looked, I saw boxes, barrels, and other forgotten possessions. Even the ubiquitous cobwebs that dangled like tattered curtains were covered with dust, clear evidence that even the spiders had abandoned the house. Overhead, I spotted a water pipe that ran through holes in the joists supporting the kitchen floor. Given the pipe's surprising height above the basement floor, it would have made a fitting location from which to hang a noose. Once again, the house corroborated Mr. Luka's description of the events.

As I toured the rest of the basement, my lantern cast shadows that danced across the white-washed stone walls. Even though the lack of footprints proved I was alone, I couldn't help feeling that I was being watched from those shadows, that something glared at me with malice and resented my intrusion into its dark domain.

Then without warning, the smell of mildew and dust made me sneeze. Strangely loud in a place that had remained silent for so many years, the sound sent a shiver down my spine. As when I was in the Paris catacombs, I had no desire to break the silence and disturb the dead. I hurriedly took my final photos and made my way back to the stairs.

Having toured the house and photographed everything that might be relevant to the TV show and the book I was writing, I brought my personal ghost-hunting equipment in from the car. I had multiple infrared and low-light cameras on tripods, motion detectors, temperature and sound recorders, and an EM frequency meter for measuring electromagnetic fluctuations and spikes. I set up my equipment in the basement, kitchen, and master bedroom. I lit a long-burning candle, the flame of which acted as a crude but sensitive way to detect changes in air currents. Then I sat down on my folding chair and waited.

By spending the night, I intended to find out for myself whether there was any truth to the Romanian folklore of demons inhabiting the bodies of the dead or the bodies of suicides turning into strigoi. Perhaps Stefan and Crina Ederescu were murdered by an ordinary human killer who took advantage of the townsfolk's superstition to blame the murders on a mythical monster. On the other hand, it was possible that Stefan and his son, Vasile, had only hallucinated the dreaded strigoi, seeing what they fearfully expected to see. In that case, Stefan and Crina's bruises could have been due to psychogenic purpura, a type of psychosomatic bruising due to extreme stress. Regardless, I intended to spend the night in the master bedroom and incorporate my experiences and the recordings from my equipment into the chapter I was writing on the haunting of the Ederescu house.

The evening slowly dragged on. The house was silent except for the rain's soft, steady pitter-patter coming in through the broken windows. Lightning occasionally lit the clouds on the western horizon, but it was too far away to hear the thunder. Ten o'clock, eleven o'clock, midnight…

I was beginning to think that nothing would happen, that I was wasting my time sitting on my folding chair in that cold and uncomfortable bedroom. But the night was still young, and there were many hours before daybreak. When, I wondered, did Omor stagger home after a night of drinking in town? Would that also be when the apparition might choose to return?

I was just beginning to doze off when I heard beeping coming from my phone. It was the ghost hunting app I wrote to connect my phone via Wi-Fi to my motion and EM detectors. The circle representing the motion detector in the basement was glowing red, while the one representing the EM frequency meter was flashing red, indicating it had detected EM spikes. Something uncanny was in the basement! I switched off the app's alarm function and waited, secure in knowing that my cameras and sound recorder were making a record of whatever it was. After several minutes, the two circles representing the basement detectors turned green, indicating that they were operational but not detecting anything.

A few minutes passed, and then the green circles representing the two detectors in the kitchen turned red. Whatever it was, it was now in the kitchen! One after another, I heard the kitchen cabinets being thrown open and then slammed shut. The red circle representing the EM meter flashed faster, indicating the EM spikes were repeating more rapidly. Then, I heard the table sliding across the floor and crashing hard into a wall. Perhaps the thing from the basement had been searching for something and hadn't found what it was looking for. Now it sounded angry. Then the two red circles representing the detectors in the kitchen turned back to green.

More minutes passed. The circle representing the bedroom EM meter turned red and began to flash. I smelled the apparition before I saw it. The faint scent of smoke slowly filled the room. Then, the smell started to change. Besides the smoke from a fire, I began to smell the stink of burning meat, as though someone had accidentally dropped a hamburger onto the hot coals of a barbeque. Finally, a third foul odor overpowered the others, one that I recognized from my tour of duty during the Iraq War: the sickening stench of death.

The temperature suddenly dropped, and the light representing the motion detector in the corner turned from green to red. Something uncanny had entered the room, but whatever it was, it was invisible to me but not to the motion detector. Then I remembered that the apparition had vanished when Stefan and Vasile Ederescu had each turned on the lights. Maybe I could only see it if the room was nearly dark. I reached over and switched off the lantern, leaving only the dim glow from a candle to illuminate the room.

There it was, just inside the broken window that looked out over the fields behind the farmhouse. A faint, vaguely human-shaped, smoky silhouette glided silently toward the bed. The ghostly apparition paused, hovering next to the empty bed as if confused by the lack of victims. Then, it advanced until it floated silently over the dust-covered bedding like a foul miasma over a stinking bog. Somehow, I seemed to sense the ghost's jumbled emotions: confusion, frustration, and overwhelming rage. But underlying them all was a cold, deep-seated malevolence, an envious hatred of all living things that moved freely under the sun.

Carefully, not daring to take my eyes off the apparition, I selected my phone's camera function. I slowly began to rotate my upper body so that I could take a picture. My chair softly creaked, just loud enough to be heard over the sound of the rain. I froze, but it was too late.

In an instant, the ghost was on me! I could feel its incorporeal fingers wrapped tightly around my throat and smell the foul reek of alcohol on its putrid breath. I tried desperately to shove the apparition off me, but I might as well have tried pushing against fog. The ghost had no such problem. Blow after painful blow struck my face and upper body, and I knew without any doubt that it hated me. If I didn't escape soon, it would surely beat me to death.

I fell off the chair, hitting my head hard on the wooden floor. My fall had knocked over the candle, snuffing out its tiny flame and throwing the room into nearly complete darkness. Above me, the ghost of smoke and vapor was gone, replaced by a dim phosphorescent phantom. Omor! I could clearly see him floating over me, his face contorted with rage, his eyes faintly glowing red as though they were windows providing a view into Hell itself. Unable to break his grip around my neck, I reached out my arms to find something, anything, that I could use as a weapon.

The lantern! I pulled it to me, found the switch, and flicked it. After hours of near-total darkness, its light was blindingly brilliant. Instantly, the invisible hands around my neck were gone. Blinking tears from my burning eyes, I looked around. The room was empty. Omor's ghost was gone!

No, not gone. It was waiting just out of sight. I could still smell its stench. The room was still cold as ice, so cold that I could see my breath. I could still feel its evil eyes watching me, just waiting for a chance to murder me like it had murdered members of its own family. But it feared the light as I feared the darkness. I was safe.

Then the light of the lantern flickered. Several seconds passed. The lantern flickered again, this time longer. Beginning to panic, I staggered up from the floor, circled the bed, and ran out into the hall. I could sense the ghost behind me, following me as I descended the stairs. The lantern's light winked out. I frantically flicked its switch off and back on, but the lantern refused to work. I felt invisible hands clutching at my back. Dropping the lantern, I bolted for the door.

Abandoning my expensive equipment, I fled to my car in a desperate race to put distance between myself and the evil miasma that had once been Omor's strigoi. As I drove back to my motel room, it became clear to me what I had to do. The next morning, I checked out of the motel, ensuring that the clerk knew I had finished my research and was returning to Pittsburgh. Then I drove out of Bogdan, heading east for Highway 69, which ran north from Indianapolis through Fort Wayne to the Ohio Turnpike that would eventually take me home. But I only traveled a few exits before turning off to stop at a gas station I could see from the highway. There I bought a cigarette lighter and three one-gallon containers of gasoline. Instead of returning to the highway, I followed the country road west to a nearby town where I found a liquor store and bought two bottles of cheap vodka. With my preparations complete, I found a nice restaurant and spent most of the day writing my book chapter on the haunting of the Ederescu house.

Around mid-afternoon, I set the rest of my plan into action. I continued west until I had driven well past Bogdan before turning south and driving down to the road that passed through the little town. By taking that circuitous route, I finally reached the Ederescu farm from the west, unobserved.

After parking behind the house so that my car wouldn't be visible from the road, I reentered the house and verified that it was empty. Then as quickly as possible, I gathered up my folding chair, lantern, and the equipment the apparition had forced me to abandon the previous night. After dousing the assorted junk cluttering the basement with one gallon of gas, I poured the second gallon around the master bedroom and the third around the kitchen. Then, I took an oil lamp from the front room and filled it with vodka. Finally, I placed the remaining bottle-and-a-half of vodka on the kitchen table. I had set the trap. The only thing left to do was to wait in my car until sunset and then lure the smoky remains of Omor's strigoi into the kitchen.

Several hours later, as the clouds along the western horizon grew dark, I exited my car. Then crouching just outside of one of the kitchen's broken windows with my lighter and oil lamp, I called out to the angry spirit of smoke and malevolence. "Omor! There's vodka in the kitchen! Come and drink your fill!"

I waited, peering over the windowsill, but nothing happened. Once more, I called out. "Omor Ederescu, come out! There's vodka in the kitchen! Come and drink!"

Then I saw it. A misty swirl of smoke rose through the floor. Faint at first, then stronger, I could smell smoke, burnt meat, and the stench of death. Slowly, lifted by invisible hands, one of the vodka bottles levitated off the table, and its contents began to disappear. I lit the alcohol-filled oil lamp and threw it through the open window. I heard it smash as I turned, then felt the intense heat of the burning alcohol and gasoline on my back as I sprinted to my car. Seconds later, I was on the road, racing west and away from Bogdan with the Ederescu house ablaze in my rearview mirror.

If fire can burn an apparition made of smoke, then the burning of the Ederescu house has finally banished Omor to an eternity in the fires of Hell. If not, then maybe I have at least deprived the strigoi of the dwelling that bound his spirit to this world. Regardless, the house will no longer pose a danger to any who might be — like I had been — drawn to it. I can only pray that no one will ever build another house on that cursed spot.

To avoid suspicion of being an arsonist, I had to maintain my fiction of having left for home before the Ederescu house was torched. So, during my first break at one of the rest stops along the road, I called the director of *Is Your House Haunted?* Though I did feel somewhat guilty for lying and for the wasted effort my lie would cause the production team, I highly recommend he base an upcoming episode on the house.

And I still planned on including a chapter on the Ederescu house in my book, *Haunted Buildings of the Midwest*. Of course, I'd naturally have to end the chapter with the house still standing, either that or with a mysterious unsolved arson.

All in all, it was a productive, if terrifying, trip. I gathered some useful information. I'd even managed to finally put an end to an evil spirit that might well murder a less careful — not to mention a less lucky — investigator.

Thus, I was pretty pleased with myself as I pulled into my driveway. I carried my luggage inside, leaving the carrying-in of my equipment for another day. I cooked a celebratory steak and sat down in front of the TV to watch *Young Frankenstein*, one of my all-time favorite movies. It wasn't until near its end that I smelled the faint stench of smoke, burning meat, and death and felt the icy grip of phantom fingers around my neck.

Author's Comments

This story resulted from my desire to write a classic ghost story. I especially enjoyed researching the Romanian superstitions associated with traditional funerals.

MADAM KALDUNYA'S DOLLS

The festive sounds of a steam calliope competed with the noise of dozens of voices talking and laughing as Ava led Isabella past the circus's sideshow. The delicious aromas of popcorn, funnel cakes, and hot dogs contrasted with the odors of sawdust and the pungent smell of the circus animals in nearby cages. Isabella paused briefly in front of each colorful wagon and tent, forcing Ava to stop and impatiently wait for her roommate to move on to the next attraction.

"Come on, Isabella," Ava insisted. "We'll never get there if you insist on stopping every ten feet."

"Ava, the circus doesn't close for another four hours," Isabella argued. "Relax and enjoy it. Your fortuneteller isn't going anywhere, and I'm going to want to watch some of these shows. The two jugglers back there were pretty good, and I'm going to want to come back and see the fire-eater's act."

The young women walked on, arm-in-arm, with Ava pulling her roommate just a bit faster than Isabella wished to go.

"What's so special about this fortuneteller anyway?" Isabella asked. "You know it's all just an act, and they don't actually know the future, right?"

"Not this one," Ava said with certainty. "You know how Robert acted last night?"

"Of course." Isabella laughed at the memory. "It was impossible not to notice. He had you up most of the night, and from the sounds coming from your bedroom, I'm amazed you can even walk today. But what's that got to do with the fortuneteller? Did she foretell an endless night of passion?"

"As a matter of fact, she did. But that wasn't from her using her crystal ball or Tarot cards. She sold me a love potion, and I sneaked some of it into his drink at dinner!"

"What?" Isabella exclaimed. "God knows what was in it. For all you know, you could have been dosing him with ecstasy or some other party drug!"

"That wasn't ecstasy, and it wasn't just the sex. Robert and I were really making love, and you saw how loving he was this morning. I had to practically push him out the door, or he would never have gone in to work."

"Well, I have to admit he was definitely different this morning than his usual boring self."

"Robert's not boring; he's dependable. Besides, what about Brad? He's been distant, hasn't been returning half your phone calls or texts, and has generally been lacking in the love department. So, I want you to get some of Madam Kaldunya's love potion and try it yourself. It may be just what he needs to wake up and realize just how good you are."

Isabella suddenly stopped. "Brad!" she hissed.

"What?" Ava asked, surprised by Isabella's stopping.

"It's Brad. He lied to me. He said he had to study for a programming certification test, but I just saw him over by that food truck."

Ava looked in the direction Isabella was pointing. "I don't see him. Are you sure it was Brad?"

"I'm sure," Isabella fumed. "And he was with Darlene Howard. He was leading her back towards those trees!"

"Damn. That sucks. But girl, as I've told you at least a dozen times, you can certainly do better. He may be handsome, but he's not exactly the sharpest knife in the kitchen. And he's got rocks for brains if he's cheating on you. Come on, Isabella, forget Brad. Let's go. I want you to meet Madam Kaldunya. She can read your fortune. Maybe Mr. Right is out there waiting for you."

Ava stopped in front of a small black tent under a banner that read "Madam Kaldunya: Fortunes Told and Made." Wearing a black hooded cape over a traditional Russian peasant dress, the fortuneteller sat behind a small table. It held the tools of her trade: a large crystal ball and a deck of ornate, antique Tarot cards. To pass the time between customers, the old woman was knitting a long, many-colored scarf, the end of which reached the floor and curled at her feet.

Madam Kaldunya looked up as Ava preceded Isabella into the tent. "Hello, Ava," the old woman said with a strong Russian accent. "Did you use the potion I gave you?"

"I did." Ava beamed.

"Yes, I thought so." The fortuneteller nodded knowingly. "And I see from your smile and the lack of sleep in your eyes that the results were most satisfying."

"Absolutely." Ava blushed under the old woman's intense gaze.

Madam Kaldunya turned her gaze on Isabella. "I sense that you are also unsatisfied with your love life." She paused for a second as a frown replaced her smile. "But with you, I see anger. Perhaps your lover has harmed you. Not physically. No. Hmm. He lied to you and was unfaithful!"

"How? How could you possibly know?" Isabella asked, shocked at the fortuneteller's insights.

"Nothing remains hidden from those of us with the Sight," the fortuneteller said. "Do you also wish a love potion to win back your lover, or is it too late for that? What is your desire: love or revenge?"

Isabella paused, torn between the two choices. "Revenge!" she finally whispered.

"Isabella," Ava said. "I know you're pissed at Brad but stop and think for a minute."

"Ava, all I've done for weeks is think about it. I'm sick of his lying and his broken promises. I'm sick of the way he makes me feel."

"Then break up with him," Ava argued.

"I *am* dumping his ass. But first, I'm going to teach him he can't treat people like this." She turned to the fortuneteller. "Do you have a potion to punish a liar who cheats on his lover?"

"No, my dear," Madam Kaldunya said. "I have something better." Getting up with great effort, the old woman slowly hobbled over to an ornate trunk in the corner of her tent. She lifted the lid and pulled out two small, crudely fashioned effigies sewn from odd patches of different colored cloth. Then returning to her seat, she sat them down on the table in front of Isabella.

"Are you sure that you want to do this?" the old woman asked. "Once done, it cannot be undone. To curse the man who betrayed you and the woman who bewitched him, are you willing to pay the price?"

Isabella stared warily at the two little effigies, one wearing simple pants and the other a dress. "What price? How much is this going to cost me?" she said, pulling her wallet out of her purse.

"I don't mean money," Kaldunya replied. "We will speak of that later. No, the price I refer to is cause and effect, action and reaction. Every spell has its cost, dark ones most of all. Sometimes, the Fates are kind; sometimes, they are cruel. A fortune such as this, I cannot foretell."

"I'll take my chances," Isabella said. "I'm the injured party. I want Brad and Darlene to pay for betraying me!"

A sudden breeze caused the tent to shudder. "The die is cast, and the Fates will decide." Kaldunya held out her hand for the payment. "That will be ten dollars. Each."

"That's kind of steep for just a couple of simple cloth dolls," Ava argued.

"Stupid girl!" Kaldunya said, glaring at Ava. "She is not buying dolls; she is buying revenge." The old woman turned back to Isabella. "Pay now or leave."

Isabella opened her purse and put two ten-dollar bills into the fortuneteller's hand.

Madam Kaldunya slid the effigies and a small pincushion holding half-a-dozen bronze needles across the table. "When you are ready, clearly envision the harm you desire and stick these needles into the associated parts of the effigies. If you believe, then the Fates will grant your wish, though perhaps not in the way you intended."

Isabella placed the dolls and pincushion into her purse, and the roommates headed out into the night.

Madam Kaldunya picked up her knitting and began once more to weave the yarn of possibilities into a web of things to come. While the Fates weaved the future from the threads of peoples' lives, Kaldunya enjoyed adding her own touch to the pattern. Isabella would choose to curse Brad *first*, and that curse would cut short the yarn of both Brad's *and* Darlene's lives. And with Darlene dead, the second curse had only one place it could go.

...

"Stop it!" Ava commanded as the roommates made their way out of the circus.

"What?" Isabella asked as she swiveled her head back and forth.

"Looking for Brad and Darlene! You know how Brad is. They're probably at his place by now. Forget the bastard. Let's head back to the apartment and get wasted. I'll make screwdrivers, and we can finish off the ice cream in the freezer."

Isabella was silent, fuming at Brad, on the drive home. Once back in their apartment, Ava got out the ice cream and added vodka to glasses of orange juice while Isabella sat on the couch. Removing the two effigies and pincushion from her purse, Isabella looked closely at each one.

"I'm going to do it," Isabella announced as Ava returned with the ice cream and drinks. "I'm going to teach Brad and Darlene for cheating on me."

"You realize they're just dolls, right?" Ava said. "That sticking pins in them won't really work; that you're just doing this to blow off some steam until you call Brad tomorrow and tell him you're done with his sorry ass."

"Maybe, maybe not. That love potion seemed real enough last night."

"Yeah, but like you said, it could have had something in it. This voodoo crap is no more real than the romantic fantasy novels you read."

"You're right," Isabella conceded, "but it's my fantasy, so stop spoiling it. Tonight, all I want to do is get drunk and pretend I can make Brad and Darlene suffer like they're making me suffer."

"Okay, roomie, tonight we drink, pig out on ice cream, and pretend. So, who are you going to curse first? Brad?"

"Of course," Isabella said as she picked up the male effigy representing Brad and four of the bronze needles. "Since you couldn't keep your eyes and hands off Darlene, I curse your eyes and your hands." She angrily stabbed the four needles into the doll's eyes and hands before hurling it hard against the wall. It dropped down, landing out of sight behind a recliner.

Then picking up the female effigy and two more needles, Isabella continued. "Darlene, the next time you're tempted to sneak off with another woman's man and break her heart, let's see how you like it when someone breaks *your* heart." She jabbed the needles into the center of the doll's chest before flinging it against the wall so that it fell down to lie next to the one that represented Brad.

"There, are you happy now?" Ava asked sympathetically.

"Not really," Isabella replied. "I thought pretending might make me feel better, but it didn't." She sighed, placing her hand over the heart that Brad had broken. "I need another screwdriver."

"Those dolls were a waste of twenty bucks, if you ask me," Ava observed. "We could have bought another bottle of vodka with that money."

Isabella was halfway to the refrigerator when she collapsed. Screaming in agony, she writhed on the floor with her face hideously contorted by pain. A few seconds later, she lay deathly still as two small spots of blood formed on her blouse.

"Isabella! No!"

...

"Morning, Aaron," Homicide Detective James Jackson said as he walked into the autopsy room at the city morgue. Having worked all night, he was in desperate need of breakfast and a strong cup of coffee, but they would have to wait.

"Hello, Jim," Dr. Edelstein, the medical examiner, replied. "You're in early this morning. You hear about the female homicide victim who arrived last night?"

"Actually, not just her. I'm also interested in the two traffic fatalities brought in at about the same time. Their car clipped a tree and dropped down into a gully up on Ridge Road. We were lucky that the driver of another car saw them leave the road. It could have been days before anyone noticed the damaged tree and realized a car was down in the gully."

"Which body do you want to see first?"

Madam Kaldunya's Dolls

"Let's start with the driver from the car wreck. I have a bet with Sergeant Jacobs that it wasn't an accident."

"You win that bet," Dr. Edelstein said with surprise as he led Detective Jackson to one of the autopsy tables. "But how in the hell did you figure that out? I was halfway through the autopsy of the driver before I determined it was a homicide."

"We arrested a suspect who told us a cockamamie story about how her roommate dropped dead after sticking pins into voodoo dolls representing the two traffic fatalities."

"Well, that's something you don't hear every day." Dr. Edelstein pulled back a sheet to reveal the partially dissected body of a young man. "Brad Turner, age 25," the medical examiner continued, reading from a clipboard. Small bloody holes in the man's palms looked like little stigmata. Dr. Edelstein had removed the top of the man's skull and placed the brain on a tray on a nearby table. "Take a look at this," he said, pulling back the man's eyelids. "Both of the man's eyes had been punctured. Have you ever seen a traffic accident damage a person's eyes like this?"

Detective Jackson shook his head.

"Me, neither," Dr. Edelstein agreed. "But that's not what convinced me it was a homicide." Gingerly picking up the victim's brain in his gloved hands, the medical examiner carefully turned it over. "See this damage on the inferior surface of each frontal lobe?" he asked, pointing to two long parallel gashes along the base of the

A Cauldron of Uncanny Dreams

brain. "These were made by a long skinny rod jammed through the victim's eyes and into his brain. They reach all the way to the back of his skull. There's no way this could happen accidentally during a car wreck. This was a homicide that happened before the crash."

"Aaron, how can you possibly know that the homicide happened before the crash? And how do you explain the fact that the victim was driving the car some 60 miles an hour when it crashed?"

"As for the answer to your first question, look at how the crash deformed the left frontal lobe. See how that caused the gash to curve while the one on the right lobe remains straight. The murder weapon produced straight gashes, one of which was then deformed during the crash," Dr. Edelstein explained. "As to your second question, thankfully, that's your job, not mine. And I'm telling you, Jim, there's no way the man could have been driving with wounds like these."

"What about his passenger? Anything unusual about her injuries?"

Dr. Edelstein led the detective to the next table. "Darlene Howard, age 21." He pulled back the sheet, uncovering the bruised body of a young woman. "There is nothing unusual as far as I can see from the outside. Looks like a dime-a-dozen traffic accident victim with lots of blunt-force trauma and superficial cuts and abrasions. I'll let you know for sure once I complete the autopsy and receive the toxicology report."

"Okay, Aaron. Let's look at the woman who was stabbed in her apartment."

"Isabella Peterson, age 23." Dr. Edelstein pulled back the sheet, revealing the upper half of the young woman's lifeless body. The autopsy was well underway. A large Y-shaped incision revealed that the sternum had been cut, and the ribs spread to show where the heart had been removed for further examination. "Now, here is where things get a little weird. The cause of death was two stab wounds through the chest and into the heart."

"Weird in what way?"

"These injuries match those of Brad Turner. In both cases, the weapon was a slender rod about an eighth of an inch in diameter. Small tears in the skin and muscles indicate the weapon's tip was rounded rather than sharp, which rules out an ice pick. In fact, I'm at a bit of a loss as to what could have caused these wounds."

"Is it possible they were caused by some kind of knitting or crochet needle?"

"I suppose a knitting needle might fit. However, the hook on a crochet needle would have caused more tearing of the tissues. Why? Did you find some at the scene?"

"Remember what I said about her roommate's crazy story? According to Ava Hansen — that's the woman who shared an apartment with Isabella Peterson — they were at the circus last night. While there, they spotted Peterson's boyfriend, Brad Turner, making out with Darlene Howard, the second victim in the car wreck. Hansen and Peterson went to a fortuneteller named…" The detective took a small notebook out of his pocket. "Madam Kaldunya, who apparently knits when she's between customers. That made me wonder whether Hansen mentioned knitting because she used a knitting needle as the murder weapon."

The detective paused briefly to gather his thoughts before continuing. "Anyway, she claims the fortuneteller sold Peterson two voodoo dolls, one representing Brad Turner and the other Darlene Howard. Peterson and Hansen then returned home to their apartment and got drunk. Then a little after 9 PM, Peterson stuck needles into the eyes and hands of the male doll…"

"Didn't I read that was when the car wreck occurred?" Dr. Edelstein asked.

"Exactly. And it was also on the opposite side of town from Peterson and Hansen's apartment. Hansen claims that after her roommate stuck two needles into the heart of the doll representing Darlene Howard, Peterson screamed and collapsed. Hansen called 911, but Peterson was dead when the EMTs arrived. That's when I was called to the scene and took Hansen's statement."

"That's quite a story," Dr. Edelstein observed. "So, Hansen and the three victims knew each other, and jealousy is definitely a motive for murder. I take it you suspect Hansen of the three murders?"

"Yes, we're holding her on suspicion of the murders of Brad Turner, Darlene Howard, and

Isabella Peterson. But several things just don't add up. What does Turner's infidelity have to do with Hansen's motive to kill her roommate? How could Hansen simultaneously kill Turner and Peterson when they were so far from each other? And finally, we haven't found the murder weapon yet. My best guess is Miss Hanson had an accomplice, who stabbed Mr. Turner and knocked out Miss Howard. Then, he put their bodies in Turner's car and somehow caused its high-speed crash. But I can't help but feel like I'm overlooking something important. I just don't know what it might be."

"Don't worry, Jim. You're a detective. You'll figure it out. You always do."

Author's Comments

The idea behind this story was the trope in which protagonists make deals with the Devil in which the Devil grants their wishes, just not in the way they expected. I wondered how a person using a voodoo doll could accidentally have their curse rebound on them. Kaldunya is a Russian word for *witch*.

BILLY THE ARSONIST

Billy Henderson liked to burn things. As far back as he could remember, he had loved to watch the flames dance. His fascination started innocently enough. As a toddler, he'd sit for hours in front of the fireplace and stare at the fire devouring the logs until only the ashes remained.

When he was nine, his dad showed him how a magnifying glass could concentrate the sun's light and set a bit of newspaper on fire. Soon, Billy was sneaking into his father's office and taking the magnifying glass outside where he could burn whatever he wanted with no one telling him no. It wasn't long before Billy discovered that he could use the magnifying glass to instantly incinerate ants and other small bugs.

By middle school, he had learned how to make huge fireballs by throwing gasoline and kerosene onto a bonfire. And by high school, he had graduated to arson.

Billy had begun small. The first building he burned had been only a shed, but soon he began torching abandoned houses. Fire had become his narcotic, and he found he needed ever-larger fires to feed his addiction.

Billy hadn't meant to kill the wino sleeping in the last building he had torched. He had been in a hurry and merely gotten sloppy, forgetting to check all the rooms. The accident — for Billy had convinced himself that a mistake could hardly count as murder — had been unexpectedly pleasurable. The old man's screams had given Billy a kind of ecstasy he found irresistible. However, the homeless man's death had made the newspapers, and the police had become far more vigilant. Billy had no choice but to stop for a while, and the wait was eating at him.

Then Billy's grandmother had died. The Pandemic had cost Billy's father his job, and the family couldn't afford a big funeral and burial. So, they had settled on a quick cremation. Billy was fascinated. He realized that if he had a job at a crematorium, he could burn bodies every day, and no one would stop him or think his fascination with fire strange. Granted, there would be no screams, but he could do without, at least for a little while until the police gave up looking for him.

Billy decided he had to try it and see for himself. That very night, he would break into the crematorium and explore the place. He would see where they stored the bodies and, most important of all, where they burned them. Billy thought that he might even burn one himself to see if cremating the dead would quell his hunger and give him the fix he craved — no, the fix he desperately needed.

Just after midnight, Billy drove to the crematorium where his grandmother's body had been incinerated. He parked behind the building to avoid being seen. Then, using a crowbar, it only took a minute to jimmy the back door.

Billy listened carefully for any sound that might indicate someone had heard him breaking in, but the building was as quiet as a crypt. Ignoring the ceremony and urn storage rooms, he crept into the mortuary cooler, the refrigerated storeroom in which the deceased patiently waited their turn in the furnace. An elderly man and a middle-aged woman lay silently on stainless-steel body trays in the frigid cold.

It didn't take long for Billy to find the furnace room where cleansing flames would feast on their flesh, reducing them to ash and scattered bits of bone. He was about to return to the cold store to select a body when he heard a chuckle, and something hard and heavy struck the back of his skull.

Billy came to with a painful headache, one far worse than he'd ever thought possible. He squeezed his eyes shut in a vain attempt to shut out the blinding light that threatened to split his head open. A hand slapped him hard across the cheek, and he cried out in pain.

"Wakey wakey, eggs and bakey," an old man's voice cheerfully sang in the way one might use with a young child. "Time to wake up and join the party!"

"No...," Billy moaned, twisting his head away from the mocking voice.

The hand slapped him again, even harder than before. "Wake up, sleepyhead. Open your eyes and join the party." Fingers roughly pulled Billy's eyelids open, and the bright light filled his eyes with tears.

The man was leaning over him, his face far too close for Billy to bring into focus.

Billy tried to push the man away, only to discover that he couldn't move his arms. He forced his eyes open and looked down. He was sitting in a wheelchair, with heavy-duty zip ties binding his wrists and forearms to its armrests. Billy tried kicking his legs, but they too were tied tightly to the chair's legrests. Ratchet straps at his chest and hips bound him so that only his head was free to move.

With his vision beginning to clear, Billy looked up at the man standing over him. He recognized him from his grandmother's funeral. It was Mr. Damian Whipple, the rotund proprietor and sole employee of Whipple's Mortuary and Crematorium. The old man looked down at Billy and smiled a predatory smile.

"Let me go!" Billy screamed, then flinched at the pain his yelling had caused his aching head.

Mr. Whipple gave Billy a quizzical look, as though actually considering his command. "No," he said, shaking his head. "I think not. I think I very much like you just the way you are."

"Damn it, let me go!" Billy commanded through clenched teeth, trying not to raise his voice and make his pounding headache any worse than it already was.

"Billy, Billy," Mr. Whipple said with a chuckle, jiggling his double chin. "I don't think you quite grasp your role in our little celebration. I stand here, as free as can be, while you, young man, are tied up quite securely. That means I am tonight's master of ceremonies and decide when the show is over."

"What do you mean by 'celebration?'" Billy asked, uneasy at the unexpected direction the old man's words were heading.

"Why Billy, you are going to join me for a very special feast, one I guarantee you'll never forget."

"Then you're not going to call the cops on me?"

"Now, why would I do that?" Mr. Whipple asked, sounding as though the thought had never occurred to him. "Certain spectacles are best performed in front of an audience of one, don't you think? Surely, given your secret proclivity, you must agree."

"What in Hell are you talking about? I don't have no proclivities, secret or otherwise."

"Why, Billy, you hurt me. You really do. Here I am about to open my heart to you, to share my deepest secrets, and you lie to me. You say you 'don't have no' secret proclivities, but you do. I know you, Billy Henderson. I know you and all your secrets."

"You don't know shit about me, old man! Either call the cops or let me go."

Billy the Arsonist

"I know ALL about you, boy. I know of your habit of starting fires when no one is watching. I know each and every fire you've set."

"But..."

"And I know about poor Mr. Johnson, who unfortunately chose to sleep off an evening of drinking in the last house you torched."

"You're wrong! That wasn't me!"

"Liar! I even know why you broke in tonight. You wanted to see if cremating a soulless body would give you the same rush you got from murdering Mr. Johnson."

"How... how could you possibly know that?"

Mr. Whipple laughed. The skin of the old man's face melted like wax in a furnace, revealing another, deeper skin that was red and pockmarked. His already fat body grew grotesquely obese, his teeth lengthened and sharpened, and two short horns emerged from his forehead.

"Billy, you thought that working at a crematorium might let you practice your pyromania safely away from prying eyes. I, too, find working here has its advantages. I can carve up the dead and feast my fill, then dispose of the evidence with no one the wiser."

"You're... you're the devil!"

"No, Billy. You are far too insignificant to merit Master's attention. I'm just a simple demon in the service of Beelzebub, doing my small part to foster the sin of gluttony while I wait for Armageddon."

A desperate thought occurred to Billy. "I'll sell you my soul. Just let me outta here."

"Billy, you think you can bargain with me?" the demon asked with a predatory smile as he rolled the young man into the cold room. "How very droll. Your soul is already destined for Hell. When I finally let you die, that's where you'll wake up."

"Please, I'll do anything…"

"Yes, of course, you would." The demon nodded his agreement before shaking his head. "But no. You need to look at it from my point of view. Day after day, they deliver nothing but the bodies of the old and sick. But old people are far too tough and stringy, while diseases spoil the meat and ruin the taste.

"You, however," the demon continued, staring hungrily at Billy, "are still young and healthy. Your body is practically begging to be eaten."

A dagger with a long, wicked blade suddenly appeared in the demon's hand. It glowed a dull red as if it had just been taken from the flames of Hell.

Billy gasped, his eyes wide with terror.

"Good," the demon said, nodding his approval. "Very good. I can smell the sweet fear in your sweat. The taste of adrenaline and cortisol will add that special something, that *je ne sais quoi*, that will make our intimate little meal truly memorable."

Billy the Arsonist

"No!" Billy interrupted.

"Yes!" the demon continued. "I think we'll begin with an appetizer of chilled tongue tartare, ground fine with raw egg yolk, diced shallot, and chopped parsley garnished with capers, olive oil, and just a dash of salt. For the entrée, let's have something simple and unassuming. How about two or three thick steaks, lightly seared to hold in the juices? And to finish, a handful of fingertips washed down with a small goblet of blood. Yes, that will make a lovely feast, don't you think?"

Billy shook his head. In fact, his whole body shook uncontrollably.

"And if I'm careful, I should be able to keep you alive and fresh for several more nights of glorious gluttony."

Billy screamed as the knife sliced his thigh to the bone. The wound sizzled as the serrated blade seared his flesh, cauterizing his femoral artery. He screamed again when the demon made his second cut, an inch above the first.

Three days later, Billy's heart eventually ceased beating, and his pain disappeared. His final thought brought a faint smile to his lips: at least, he could spend all eternity watching the fabled fires of Hell.

But Billy didn't know that Hell had its own special damnation for arsonists. When he awoke, it was in a tiny, pitch-black cell deep in the Ice Dungeon of Tartarus. For Billy, it will always be a cold, dark day in Hell.

A Cauldron of Uncanny Dreams

Author's Comments

I once wrote a short story about a ghoul who gets a job at a crematorium, where he could dine to his heart's content. That naturally led me to wonder what a psychopathic arsonist might think of the job.

A MOTHER'S GRIEF

The phone on Gary Henderson's nightstand rang, waking him from a deep sleep. He rolled over, groaned, and picked up his phone. It was 2:34 in the morning.

"Not again," Gary muttered.

"Who is it?" his wife asked.

"It's Saint Margaret's Retirement Home."

"Then you'd better answer it," she said. "You know they'll keep calling until you do."

Sighing with resignation, Gary reluctantly accepted the call. "Yes?"

"Mr. Henderson, I'm sorry to bother you again, but you need to come down right away. It's your mother," the night nurse said.

"Okay," Gary answered. "I'll get dressed and be there as soon as I can." Ending the call, he groaned again before rolling out of bed. He turned on the lights and began dressing in the work clothes he'd laid out for the morning.

"You've got to do something about this," his wife said.

"I know, Dear. I just don't know how."

"Well, you'd better think of something, or we'll never get another decent night's sleep. She's your mother. You'll just have to talk her into moving on."

Twenty minutes later, Gary pulled into the retirement home's parking lot. The lobby lights were on, and the night nurse was waiting for him. She escorted him to his mother's small suite, which he entered, closing the door behind him.

His mother sat on the couch in her tiny living room. She looked up at him with eyes red and puffy from crying. "Hello, Gary," she said and gave him a sad smile. "I'm glad you stopped by. I've felt so alone since your father died, and I just can't seem to stop crying."

"I know, Mom," Gary said and sighed, sitting down next to her. "The night nurse called me. Your crying has been waking the residents in the neighboring rooms. You're upsetting them, and some have even asked the administrator to move them to a different floor. This can't continue."

"I know," she replied. "But I miss your dad so much. Ever since Henry died, I've felt so empty and cold. My heart's broken, and I don't know how to fix it."

"I understand, Mom. I miss Dad, too. But you can't go on like this. You just have to let go and move on."

"Move on?" she asked, shaking her head at the idea. "How can you expect me to move on? I know it sounds corny, but your dad was my one true love. How can I possibly move on to someone else? Gary, how can you even suggest such a thing?"

A Mother's Grief

"Mom, I didn't mean to move on to someone else. I meant it's time for you to move on…" He paused, searching for the right words. "It's time to move on to a different place."

"Another place? How will my moving out of Saint Margaret's possibly help? Moving won't bring your father back."

"I know, Mom. But there is a way for you to be together again…" He paused, again trying to find the right words to say. "Perhaps you can be together in Heaven."

She stared at her son with a look of horror. "You… you can't mean suicide!" she exclaimed, rapidly turning to look at the large cross hanging on the opposite wall. "That's a mortal sin!"

"Of course not, Mom. That's not at all what I meant." He reached out to take her hand, doing his best to ignore the icy cold sensation as his hand passed effortlessly into hers. "I will miss you, but Dad's been waiting for you. It's time for us to say goodbye. It's time for you to go into the light and join him on the other side."

She looked down at his hand inside hers with an expression of shocked disbelief on her face. "But…"

"It's okay, Mom. A week ago, you passed peacefully in your sleep. I should have told you the first time the night nurse called me to say you'd returned, but I was too shocked to tell you. Since then, you've been returning every night, and your crying is terrifying the other residents. They've even talked to the priest about performing an exorcism."

"An exorcism?" she asked, shocked and alarmed at the idea.

Gary nodded. "Don't you think it would be best if you just let go?"

The truth slowly dawned on her. She silently nodded and gazed up into the ethereal light shining down on her. Then, she dissolved into a mist that drifted heavenward to vanish through the ceiling.

"Goodbye, Mom," he whispered, wiping the tears from his eyes. "Tell Dad that I miss him, too."

Author's Comments

This is another short story documenting a dream I had. I based the setting on the location of my mother-in-law's death.

A MOTHER'S LOVE

It was supposed to be an ordinary Friday evening. After dinner, my mom and dad left to pick up some groceries, while I stayed home to watch a horror movie. They were only going to be gone for an hour, but one hour became two, then three, and then four. I wasn't concerned. Their continued absence merely meant I could watch a second movie.

I'd just started my third movie when the doorbell rang. Getting up to see who it was, I glanced out the window and was surprised to see a police car parked in our driveway. It was unexpected, but I was more curious than concerned when I opened the door.

The police officer standing in front of the porch said, "Hello, son. Is it okay if I come in?"

"I guess so," I replied, wondering why a cop would want to talk to my parents. "My mom and dad aren't here, but they should be back soon."

He stepped inside and closed the door behind him. "What's your name?" he asked as he glanced around the room.

"Ethan, sir," I answered. "Ethan Simmons."

"Well, Ethan, is there anyone else here with you tonight?"

"No. Just me," I replied, beginning to feel a bit uncomfortable. After watching two horror movies,

I suddenly realized telling a stranger you're alone in an isolated farmhouse at least a quarter mile from your nearest neighbor usually ends badly. I had also watched enough movies to know that just because someone was a police officer didn't mean he wasn't also a mass murderer.

I followed him into the front room, and he turned off the TV. "Take a seat, Ethan," he said, pointing to the couch.

I glanced at the pistol at his hip and did as he said.

"Ethan, do you have any relatives that I can call?"

"No, sir," I answered, confused by the unexpected question. "Just Mom and Dad." I took my phone out of my pocket and started to unlock it. "I can call them if you want."

"That won't be necessary, Ethan." He looked down and sighed before continuing. "I'm afraid I have bad news. Your mom and dad were in a car crash."

"What?" I asked, suddenly upset that the police officer was wasting time with stupid questions when he should be racing me to the hospital. "Are you here to take me to them?"

"No, son. I hate having to tell you this, but your parents didn't survive the accident."

I couldn't believe it. I just couldn't. It had to be a mistake. He had to have mixed up my parents with someone else.

A Mother's Love

"Are you sure there isn't a relative I can call?" he asked as I sat there, in a state of confused denial.

When I didn't answer, he asked me again, yanking me back to a reality I couldn't accept.

"No," I eventually answered, looking up at him through eyes blurry from tears. "I'm an only child. My grandparents are dead, and I don't have any aunts or uncles." It dawned on me I was an orphan, and I realized nothing would ever be the same again. I was all alone, with no idea what was going to happen to me.

I barely heard him use his radio to talk to someone at dispatch. Then he sat down next to me.

"Ethan, look at me."

I turned to face him.

"Dispatch is contacting Child Protective Services," he said, his voice filled with pity. "The social worker on call should be here shortly, and I'll stay with you until they arrive."

"I want to see my mom and dad," I said. I didn't just want to see them. I *needed* to see them, to convince myself that they were truly dead.

"I'm afraid that won't be possible," he replied. "A tanker truck going in the opposite direction veered into their lane, and the head-on collision crushed both vehicles. The truck was hauling gasoline, and the resulting fire pretty much destroyed everything that could burn. To identify your parents, we had to use your car's license plate and the ID we found in what was left of your father's wallet. Believe me, son, it's better if you never see their bodies."

"They burned to death?" I asked in horror.

"No, Ethan. Thankfully, your parents were spared that. We're sure that it was the collision that killed them. They didn't suffer; it was over in the blink of an eye."

I may not have seen their bodies, but I'd seen enough horror movies and documentaries showing the horrors of wars. I clearly envisioned their horrendously burned bodies in the charred crumpled remains of our car. Suddenly, I found myself leaning into the police officer. He placed his arm protectively around my shoulders, and I sobbed uncontrollably against his chest.

Sometime later, after I had no more tears to cry, I heard the doorbell ring. The police officer got up and walked to the door, while I sat there, numbly wondering if there had been anything I could have done to prevent the accident. If I had only gone with them, our car wouldn't have been at the crash site at the exact instant when the tanker truck veered out of its lane. My selfish desire to stay home and watch movies was why my parents were dead.

"Ethan."

I looked up to see a middle-aged woman holding a notebook. She gazed back at me with sympathetic eyes.

A Mother's Love

"My name is Mrs. Carrington. I'm a caseworker with Child Protective Services, and I'll be taking care of you. Officer Meyer has explained to me what happened to your parents. Now that I'm here, he'll be getting back to work."

I glanced up at the police officer. I realized I didn't want him to leave, as though his mere presence could somehow protect me from what was to come.

"I'm truly sorry about your parents, Ethan," he said. "I know it doesn't feel that way now, but you'll get through this. There'll be people to help you so that you won't have to face this alone." Then he turned and walked out of the room. I would never see him again.

"Ethan," Mrs. Carrington said, regaining my attention. "In a little while, I'll take you to a nice lady who'll take care of you until I can find a more long-term place for you. We'll talk again tomorrow, but right now I do need to ask you a few questions, so I can get your casework started. Would that be okay?"

"I guess so," I mumbled in a dull monotone. The sooner I answered her questions, the sooner I could return to my dark thoughts.

She opened her notebook and picked up a pen to record my answers. "What is your full name?"

"Ethan Michael Simmons," I replied.

She wrote down my name. "And what is your birthday, Ethan?"

I told her.

"That makes you fourteen," she observed as she recorded my birthday.

I nodded, remembering that I'd be fifteen in a couple of months. Without my parents, there would be no birthday party. I didn't know if I'd ever celebrate my birthday again.

"And your parents are Elizabeth and Aaron Simmons?"

"Yes."

"Officer Meyer told me you don't have any relatives. So, no brothers or sisters? No grandparents? No aunts, uncles, or cousins."

"No, ma'am."

"And do you have to take any medications?"

"No," I replied, confused by the unexpected question.

"Good," she said as she closed her notebook. "That simplifies things. That's enough questions for tonight. Let's go up to your bedroom and pick up your PJs and some clothes for tomorrow. Then, you can grab your toothbrush. Don't worry about anything else tonight; we'll come back tomorrow for more of your clothes and other belongings."

I led her upstairs to my bedroom, where I stuffed some clothes into my backpack. I noticed the cord to my phone's charger on my nightstand and added it before heading to the bathroom for my toothbrush. As we walked back down the stairs, I spotted a small picture hanging on the wall

A Mother's Love

of Mom, Dad, and me. I grabbed it as I went by and added it to my backpack's meager collection of belongings.

"Okay, Ethan. Do you have a house key?"

"Yes," I replied. I went to the kitchen, where I knew my parents kept our spare set of keys. I paused briefly when spotting our car key reminded me it was destroyed, and my parents were dead. Handing the keys to Mrs. Carrington, I grabbed my jacket from the coat rack by the door and followed her outside. She locked the front door behind us and led me to her car.

I don't remember much about the drive into town. We eventually stopped in front of a two-story house that looked like most of the other houses on the street. I followed Mrs. Carrington up to the front door, and she rang the doorbell.

A woman a few years older than Mom opened the door. She wore a faded pink bathrobe and had the sleepy look of someone who had just been woken from a deep sleep. She glanced at Mrs. Carrington and then turned to stare at me with curiosity.

"Ethan, this is Mrs. Jackson," Mrs. Carrington said. "You'll be staying with her temporarily until I can find you a more permanent home." She turned to the woman and continued, "Janice, this is Ethan Simmons."

"Hello, Ethan," Mrs. Jackson said. "Hello, Beatrice. Come on in." She led us into the dining room, and we took seats at the large table.

Mrs. Carrington immediately took charge of the conversation. "Ethan's parents were killed in an automobile accident a few hours ago, and he has no relatives he can go to."

"I'm so sorry, Ethan," Mrs. Jackson said sympathetically. "I understand that this whole evening must seem like a horrible nightmare, and the next few weeks will be very difficult for you. But I want you to understand that you'll get through this challenging time. I know because I've cared for quite a few children who've lost their parents. You are stronger than you think, and we are here to help and support you. You might even come out stronger on the other side."

Stronger? I couldn't imagine how losing my parents would do anything but leave me broken and lonely.

Mrs. Jackson glanced up at the clock on the wall. I followed her gaze and noted it was nearing midnight. "It's getting late," she continued. Bedtime here is ten o'clock, and the other children should all be asleep by now. Let's get you settled in for the night. I'm afraid we're kind of crowded this month, so you'll have to share a room with another boy. But don't worry; Matt won't mind. He's used to sharing."

Mrs. Jackson stood, and I got up to follow her. "Give me a few minutes, Beatrice," she said to my caseworker. "I'll get Ethan settled in, and then we can take care of the paperwork. I'm sure you want to go home and get some sleep before you have to get back up and head to work in the morning."

A Mother's Love

"Good night, Ethan," Mrs. Carrington said. "I'll be back in the early afternoon to pick you up."

I grabbed my backpack and followed Mrs. Jackson up the stairs. Dozens of photographs lined the walls, presumably of the children who had passed through her care.

Stopping outside one of the doors, she turned to me and spoke softly. "This will be your bedroom, and the bathroom is at the end of the hall. Breakfast is at eight, so I'll be getting everyone up at seven-thirty." She paused for a second, then continued. "Matt also lost his parents a few weeks ago when their house burned down. He's been having nightmares, so don't be surprised if you hear him cry out. Just stay quiet and let him go back to sleep. If the two of you start talking, you'll both have trouble getting up in time for breakfast."

She opened the bedroom door. In the dim illumination of a nightlight, I could see Matt's form huddled under his blanket. The neatly made bed along the opposite wall waited silently for me. I quietly changed into my pajamas and then stopped by the bathroom to brush my teeth. Once back in the bedroom, I crawled into the strange bed. I had been afraid I wouldn't be able to sleep, but as I stared up at the ceiling, I realized just how totally exhausted I was, both mentally and physically. Within minutes, I was sound asleep.

The next morning, a knock on the door woke Matt and me.

"Who are you?" he asked groggily as he got up. It clearly surprised him to see me getting out of a bed that had been empty when he'd gone to sleep.

"Ethan," I answered. "You were already asleep when I arrived," I added, stupidly stating the obvious.

"Oh," he said, changing out of his pajamas and into his clothes. "I'm Matt. My parents died in a fire. What's your story?"

"My mom and dad were killed in a car crash yesterday evening."

He nodded glumly. "We're all orphans here," he continued. "Except for Jason. He doesn't like to talk about it 'cause his parents were busted for selling drugs."

A bell rang out.

"That's the breakfast bell. You'd better hurry and get dressed. Mrs. Jackson doesn't like being kept waiting." Then he turned and hurried out the door.

A few minutes later, I was heading down the stairs. Mrs. Jackson and five other kids, three boys and two girls, were already sitting around the breakfast table. I joined them, and Mrs. Jackson said, "Okay, let's eat." We passed around a big bowl of scrambled eggs, a plate of buttered toast, and a platter with what had to be an entire package of undercooked bacon.

Breakfast was an awkward affair with Mrs. Jackson trying valiantly to keep the conversation going. With it still being summer, there was no school. One by one, she asked us how we intended to spend the day, and we each gave the shortest possible answer before lapsing back into painful silence. It was blatantly obvious we were all seriously broken, and nothing she could say could possibly fix us. Eventually, she gave up, and we finished eating in silence. Some of us migrated to the living room to watch TV, while the rest found quiet places to sit, took out their phones, and lost themselves in surfing the internet, watching videos, or listening to music. I just wanted to be left alone, so I went back up to the bedroom. I had plenty of dark thoughts to keep me occupied while I waited for lunch and for my caseworker to come and pick me up.

Lunch was spaghetti with a bland, tasteless tomato sauce that was nothing like the thick meaty one my mother made that she flavored with onions, garlic, and fresh herbs from our garden. Everything seemed to remind me of my parents as their absence ate at my soul. And it wasn't only me. No matter how much Mrs. Jackson tried to cheer us up, sadness and depression permeated the house, hanging in the air like a dark and evil fog.

Eventually, Mrs. Carrington, my caseworker, arrived to drive me back home to gather more of my stuff. Once we were alone in her car, she turned to me and said, "Ethan, I have some very good news."

Good? What news could possibly be good? Unless my parents had miraculously risen from the dead, I seriously doubted there could be any news that I'd consider good. "What news?" I asked warily.

"As I was researching your family this morning, I discovered that you actually do have close relatives."

"What?" I asked, dumbfounded by the news. "Mom and Dad told me my grandparents had died when they were teenagers and that they didn't have any brothers or sisters."

"It turns out that your mother does have a sister. Your Aunt Agnes and her three children live out west in Washington state. They live in a little town up in the Cascade Range south of Mount Rainier called Cascade Peaks."

It would be a huge understatement to say I was surprised. Why, I wondered, had Mom and Dad never mentioned my Aunt Agnes? "Are you sure about me having an aunt?"

"I am," Mrs. Carrington replied. "I called her and verified that she's your mom's sister. When your maternal grandfather and grandmother divorced, your mom and aunt were only five and seven years old. Your grandparents divided their two daughters between them. Your grandfather moved to Washington, where he raised your Aunt Agnes, while your grandmother raised your mother here in Indiana. That's how your mother and your aunt became separated before you were born. It's also why your aunt didn't know her sister was married and had a son, just like you didn't know about her and her children."

A Mother's Love

"Okay," I said, unsure where the conversation was going. "But how is any of this good news?" After all, it was not as if I were her favorite nephew, and she'd love for me to come live with her.

"Well, she was sorry to learn your parents had died, and you'd been orphaned by the accident. I think there's a good chance she might be willing to have you come out and live with her and her children. If she does, it will certainly be better than having you move into an overcrowded foster home. Your odds of being adopted are very low at your age, and this could be your only chance of having a family."

"But why would my aunt take me in if she and Mom weren't close? I'm just a stranger to her."

"She did ask for a day to make up her mind," Mrs. Carrington admitted. "And taking responsibility for raising a child is a huge commitment. But, Ethan, sometimes blood really is thicker than water. I have a good feeling that she's going to say yes."

That was a lot to take in, and I really didn't know what to think. Still, I thought about how depressing Mrs. Jackson's house was with so many kids without parents. Surely, going to live with my aunt had to be better than that.

We arrived back home, and Mrs. Carrington sent me upstairs to pack a suitcase full of clothes and any other necessities I might need. I had just finished up when I heard her phone ring. Busy with the difficult job of deciding what to take and what to leave for later, I didn't pay any attention to her conversation.

Mrs. Carrington walked into my bedroom with a big smile on her face. "Great news, Ethan. That was your Aunt Agnes. She's agreed to have you move in with them!"

That was a surprise, and I didn't quite know what to think. Mrs. Carrington felt that my living with my aunt and her three children would be a lot better than my being placed in a foster home. But would it? I knew nothing about Aunt Agnes. Would she be kind to me, or would I be like Cinderella, no more than a slave to her and her children? Moving to the west coast would change my life forever, and I really had no idea if that was the best choice for me.

"What do you know about my aunt and cousins?" I asked.

"Very little, actually," she replied. "Your aunt told me that her husband died seven years ago. And that your cousin Connor is twelve, Anna is ten, and Jonathon is eight. Their house is about a mile outside of Cascade Peaks in the Gifford Pinchot National Forest. The town only has about fifty residents, even less during the winter when the summer tourists are gone. Since the nearest school is over thirty miles away, your aunt homeschools your cousins. And that's about all I've learned so far."

"That's not much," I said. I had so many questions.

A Mother's Love

"Don't worry, Ethan. I'll find out more before I send you to them. There's still a lot to do before you can go. I'll need to arrange the funeral. I've already talked to a lawyer, who will take care of selling your farm. He'll set up a trust fund for you to inherit when you turn eighteen, and he'll also send some of the money to your aunt each month to help cover your expenses."

And so, the decision was made. I would leave my family's Indiana farm for the heavily forested wilderness of the Cascade Range. Since my parents had never seemed to have the money for big vacations, I'd never been farther than a day's drive from our farm. The move out west would be an adventure; I just didn't know what kind. Would I be the hero who overcomes terrible obstacles to live happily ever after, or would my new life end up being a horror story?

The following week rushed by. The day of my parents' closed casket funeral and burial turned out to be as hard and awful as I imagined it would be. I had hoped that my aunt would be there, so I could find out what type of person she was, but apparently, she wasn't able to attend. The rest of the days were taken up by going through the house, deciding what to keep, what to sell, and what to give away. I called my friends, and we promised to stay in touch through email and social media. There was also a surprising amount of official paperwork, which my caseworker and the lawyer took care of. It left little for me to do besides signing some documents I didn't fully understand. Each evening, I returned to Mrs. Jackson's foster home to sleep in the bedroom I shared with Matt. The group meals remained stressful, and no one seemed interested in becoming friends, especially with a boy who would soon be gone.

Eventually, the day came to leave for my new home. I said goodbye to Mrs. Jackson and the other kids, and Mrs. Carrington drove me and my three suitcases to the airport for my first airplane flight. She escorted me inside, where I picked up my ticket and dropped off my luggage.

At the security check-in, we stopped to say goodbye. "Ethan, here's one hundred dollars from your trust fund to tide you over until you arrive in Tacoma. And here's my card with my phone number. Call me if you have any problems. Mr. Hansen, your new caseworker, will meet you at the airport and drive you to your new home. He'll be holding up a sign with your name on it, and I sent him your picture, so he'll recognize you."

"Okay," I said, placing the money and card into my wallet. I guess my tone and expression betrayed just how nervous and uncertain I felt at leaving Indiana.

"Don't worry Ethan. I've spent a lot of time talking to your Aunt Agnes over the last week, and she seems like a very nice person. I'm sure she'll take good care of you and that everything will all work out just fine." She glanced at her watch. "You only have about forty-five minutes before

A Mother's Love

your flight, so you'd better get to the gate for check-in."

So, we said our goodbyes, and I watched her walk away until she was out of sight. Then I turned, went through the security screening, and started on my journey to a new life with my new family. Despite Mrs. Carrington's assurance, all I could think about was that I'd be a stranger living among strangers in a strange place far from home.

I found my gate easily enough. As an unaccompanied minor, the agent had me board the airplane with the first-class passengers. I was happy to discover that I had a window seat. I even managed to spot our farm as the airplane climbed away from the airport. But the sight only reminded me that the old farmhouse wasn't really home, not anymore. Soon, the lawyer would sell it, a new family would move in, and I'd likely never see it again.

The first flight from Fort Wayne, Indiana to Chicago was so short that we had barely reached cruising altitude before the plane began its descent into O'Hare Airport. Once we landed, we must have taxied past dozens of planes before reaching the right gate. I had heard that O'Hare was larger than Fort Wayne's airport, but I didn't realize just how huge it was until then. *How am I going to find my way to my next gate?* I wondered. I only had a little over half an hour before my next flight, and I didn't even know what terminal my plane to Tacoma, Washington was leaving from.

A Cauldron of Uncanny Dreams

I needn't have worried. Being an unaccompanied minor, a flight attendant escorted me off the plane and turned me over to a waiting airline representative. He had me climb aboard a little electric cart and drove me straight to my next gate. As we weaved in and out through the thick swarm of people busily hurrying in every direction, all I could think of was how lucky I was that I didn't have to run to catch my second, longer flight.

Once we were airborne, I spent a lot of time looking out at the clouds and down at the countryside that slowly rolled beneath me. They served us lunch, and I watched a movie on the tiny screen in the back of the seat in front of me. Eventually, we flew over the Rocky Mountains and then the Cascade Range where Aunt Agnes lived. I also spotted the snow-covered peak of Mount Rainier rising high above mile after mile of unbroken forest.

Once we landed, another airline representative met me at the gate and drove me to the place where family and friends had gathered to greet the new arrivals. I spotted a man holding up a sign with my name on it. He must have recognized me from the picture Mrs. Carrington had sent him and waved to me.

"There's my ride," I told the driver of the electric cart and walked over to the man with the sign.

"Hello, Ethan," he said. "I'm Mr. Hansen. I will be your new caseworker. How was your flight?"

A Mother's Love

"Okay, I guess," I answered, not having any experience to compare it with. "Are you going to be the one who's taking me to my Aunt Agnes?"

"I am," he replied. "Now, let's go get your luggage and get on the road. It's a long drive out to Cascade Peaks."

We picked up my three suitcases and headed off to my new home. After stopping at a drive-through for a quick late lunch or early dinner, we left the city behind us and entered the foothills surrounding Mount Rainier. Everywhere I looked, there was nothing but countless evergreen trees. They reminded me of when I used to go with Dad to pick out our family Christmas tree and spend time with Mom decorating it. Something about the endless forest called to me. Before long, I could hardly wait for the two-and-a-half-hour drive to be over, so I could go exploring.

On arriving at Cascade Peaks, I learned it wasn't really a town at all. Instead, it was only a seasonal campground, where a few families lived in mobile homes all year long. Mr. Hansen talked to the owners and learned that Aunt Agnes was a bit of a recluse who lived a few miles out of town at the end of an old gravel logging road. The directions they gave us were confusing, mainly because there were no street signs on the mountain roads. Still, after a few false turns, we pulled up in front of a century-old, two-story house that had seen better days. The paint was peeling off its wooden siding, and the yard had been left to return to its natural state. I had to admit the place looked a little spooky and anything but inviting. But having come so far, there was no turning back. Besides, a small satellite dish next to the house implied they had TV and internet access.

Mr. Hansen and I unloaded my suitcases and carried them up to the front door. He had to knock several times, but my cousin Anna eventually opened the door. She looked at me, turned, and called out, "Mom, he's here!"

Anna gave me the distinct impression that she was ill, but from what I couldn't guess. Framed by long black hair, Anna's round face was almost ghostly white. It looked as though she seldom, if ever, ventured out into the sun. She also had dark rings under her eyes that were even more noticeable because of the paleness of her skin.

My Aunt Agnes came to the door, and Anna stepped to the side. While my cousin was more than a little chubby, my Aunt Agnes looked like she was starving to death. Her sunken cheeks and deep-set eyes gave her face a skull-like appearance, and she was so emaciated that her arms and hands seemed little more than skin over bones. My aunt was unnaturally pale like her daughter, and her thinning gray hair hung limply on her bony shoulders. She also looked old enough to be my grandmother instead of my aunt. I didn't know what I had expected my aunt to look like, but this definitely wasn't it.

Nevertheless, Aunt Agnes gave us a warm smile and opened the door wide to let us in. "Welcome, Ethan, Mr. Hansen. Come in, come in."

My social worker and I stepped inside, leaving my suitcases on her front porch.

"Let me look at you, Ethan," Aunt Agnes continued. "What a fine-looking young man you are. I wasn't sure I believed Mrs. Carrington when she called and told me I had a nephew. But it's clear you're Lizzie's boy. You have our family's ears."

I glanced at my aunt's ears and saw the same little bump of cartilage I shared with my mom. It was the reason some of my friends gave me the nickname Elf. Unfortunately, it's also why some of the school bullies liked to call me 'Fairy' Simmons.

Leaning down, Aunt Agnes gave me a bony hug. Her cool skin gave off the faint smell you sometimes get from old people or someone who's been sick a very long time. Then, she ushered us into the front room, where Connor and Jonathon sat on the couch watching TV. The boys looked a lot like their sister, chubby with round faces nearly as pale as the white grubs that sometimes infested our corn crops.

"Connor and Jonathon, come and say hello to your cousin, Ethan."

The boys struggled to their feet and slowly shuffled over to say hello, and Aunt Agnes laid her hand lovingly on their shoulders. "I'm sure the four of you will get along splendidly. Why, you'll be thick as thieves in no time at all."

I had my doubts but kept them to myself. Looking at my cousins, wondering what we could possibly have in common. I spent as much time outdoors as I could and loved to go hiking in the nearby woods when I'd finished my chores. Unfortunately, my three cousins looked like their idea of a walk was a trip to the kitchen for something to eat. Still, maybe I could convince Connor to at least go for short walks.

My three cousins stared at me with the same curiosity with which I looked back at them. I had no idea what to expect before I arrived. But I certainly hadn't expected the children to look so different from their mother and yet so strangely similar. Although I had long since stopped believing in fairy tales, I couldn't help thinking of the skeletal witch fattening up Hansel and Gretel before eating them. I forced the mental image from my mind. Aunt Agnes had been nothing but kind to me, letting me come live with her.

Before the social worker left, he accompanied Aunt Agnes and me upstairs to inspect my new bedroom. Twice, the stairs creaked loudly as I stepped on what must have been loose boards. My room was small but clean, with a window looking out over the endless forest of fir, spruce, and pine trees. While Mr. Hansen had Aunt Agnes sign some documents from my family's lawyer, I carried my suitcases upstairs and began to unpack my meager belongings. After putting my clothes in

A Mother's Love

the closet and dresser, I placed my small collection of books on an empty bookshelf and my parents' photograph on a small desk where I could do my homework. In a few minutes, I had turned the empty room into a place I could begin to call my own.

I went downstairs and found my three cousins watching TV. Mr. Hansen had left, and my aunt was in the kitchen fixing dinner.

"Aunt Agnes, can I go outside?" I asked. "I'd like to walk around and do a little exploring."

Aunt Agnes looked up and smiled. "Of course, Ethan. Just don't go too far. I'll have dinner ready in about an hour, so stay close enough to hear me when I call."

"Okay. Since I don't know the area, would it be okay if I asked Connor if he wants to come and show me around?"

Aunt Agnes shook her head sadly. "I'm afraid you'll have to go by yourself. Unfortunately, the children and I suffer from photodermatitis, which pretty much forces us to stay indoors during the day."

"What's that?" I asked, having never heard the word before.

"You might say we're allergic to sunlight. If we're out in the sun for more than a minute or two, we get terrible rashes. And if we stay out long enough, we can get quite sick."

"Oh. So, is that why you're all so pale?" I asked, before realizing the question might have been too personal.

"That's part of the reason," she replied. "We also have idiopathic iron-deficiency anemia." She noticed my look of confusion and explained, "The doctors say we don't have sufficient iron to make enough red blood cells. 'Idiopathic' is just their fancy way of saying they don't know what causes it."

"That's terrible," I said. "Isn't there anything the doctors can do about it?"

"Not really. We all take iron supplements, and I do my best to fix lots of iron-rich foods. It keeps us out of the hospital, but that's about all. As it is, you'll find we get tired and out of breath after the least bit of exercise, and it's pretty much all I can manage to do the laundry, cook, and take care of the dirty dishes. I'm afraid that now that you're here, we'll have to rely on you doing most of the heavy chores. I realize that's not fair to you, but we really do need your help."

"Don't worry, Aunt Agnes," I said. "I'll help as much as I can." I didn't like hearing that I'd get stuck with most of the chores while my cousins sat and watched TV, but what could I do? My aunt had invited me into her home, giving me a place to stay when I desperately needed one. And they were family. I figured I'd learn soon enough what my new life would be like. In the meantime, I just wanted to get out of the house and explore.

A Mother's Love

Heading out the back door, I was surprised to see a chicken coop and about twenty chickens protected by a high fence made of chicken wire attached to sturdy steel fence posts. Maybe one of my chores would be feeding the chickens and collecting their eggs. That wouldn't be so bad; it might even be fun.

Next to the chicken coop was a fenced-in area holding a huge hog that eyed me hungrily. It had probably expected me to be bringing it food.

There was also a big tool shed. I glanced inside, and from the dust and cobwebs, it looked like no one had been inside it for years. Behind the shed, I found a deer trail leading into the forest and up the hill. Following the path, I soon came to a clearing where I could look down on the Cascade Peaks Camping Grounds and the Cowlitz River that it bordered.

Unlike the muddy water of northern Indiana's rivers and streams, the river's water was so clear I was sure I'd be able to see fish from the banks. Remembering the fun my dad and I had when he took me fishing at a friend's pond, I wondered if my uncle had often gone fishing. I sighed at the bittersweet memory. Then I thought, maybe I could find his old fishing rod and tackle box lying forgotten in the shed or possibly the attic.

I took a couple of pictures with my phone and noticed that the hour my aunt had given me was nearly up. So, I headed back down the path and was almost back at the house when I heard Anna calling me in for supper. After washing my hands, I joined the others at the dining room table.

I could hardly believe my eyes. My aunt had loaded the table with a feast worthy of a Thanksgiving or Christmas dinner. There was fried liver (which I didn't like), roast beef (which I did), fried chicken, mashed potatoes, green and kidney beans, and homemade biscuits with apricot jam. "Aunt Agnes, you didn't have to fix all this food just for me."

"Oh, I didn't, dear boy," she replied as my cousins piled their plates high with food. "I always set a good table. It may be a lot of work, but I've done it ever since my husband Frank got sick, and it's become a family tradition." Aunt Agnes glanced sadly over at a picture on the wall. She and a man I took to be my uncle stared morosely out of the photo. They were both pale and skeletally thin.

"Oh?" I said, rapidly looking away from the picture. I didn't want to pry, but I was curious about my uncle. I knew next to nothing about him, though he obviously suffered from the same illness as my aunt.

"Papa died not long after Jonathon was born," Connor said sadly.

"I'm sorry," I said, feeling uncomfortable.

"That's okay," Connor said. "Anna and I barely remember him, and Colin doesn't remember him at all. The only memory I have is of how skinny he was."

A Mother's Love

I was getting really uncomfortable with where the conversation was going. Since my aunt was so emaciated, I couldn't help believing my aunt and uncle both had the same deadly disease. Was it something I could catch? But then, I looked at my cousins, who were all more than merely chubby. Whatever it was, they clearly hadn't caught it, so I figured I probably wouldn't either.

Aunt Agnes must have noticed my anxious expression when I stared at her. "Don't worry, Ethan. While the doctors don't know the cause of what Frank and I have, they've assured me it's not contagious. As you can see, I haven't put any of this wonderful food on my plate. Unfortunately, I have a great deal of difficulty digesting solid food. If I try, I get terrible stomach cramps and end up rushing to the bathroom. I'm afraid my diet consists of meat broths, apple juice, and far too many cans of cola and other sugary sodas. I'm always hungry, but I must carry on. My children have lost their father. I can't let them lose me, too."

I wondered if my aunt's tradition of cooking so much food was because she thought stuffing my cousins with food would prevent them from ending up as emaciated as she was. Still, it was hard to watch my cousins chowing down second and even third helpings. And Aunt Agnes constantly encouraged them, passing the food around any time one of their plates developed space for more.

A Cauldron of Uncanny Dreams

The food was good, and I had plenty to eat. In fact, I couldn't help eating more than I should have. While we ate, Aunt Agnes and her children peppered me with questions.

"What is Indiana like?" Colin asked.

"Flat. Cold in the winter and hot in summer," I answered between mouthfuls.

"What was it like living on a farm?" Jonathon wanted to know.

"I liked it, even though there were always lots of chores to do."

"What crops did you grow?" Aunt Agnes enquired.

"Corn and soybeans."

"What did you like to watch on TV?" Anna asked.

"Science fiction, fantasy, and horror," I said. "I like both movies and series."

I also asked them lots of questions. Although it was late summer, so there was no school, I still wanted to know what it was like to be homeschooled. Until school started, my cousins' typical days mostly consisted of watching TV and eating, although my aunt did encourage everyone to read at least one book a week. I also learned Aunt Agnes didn't have a job because of her illness. Instead, they lived off my uncle's life insurance money, her disability payments, and SNAP food assistance. It was clear that Aunt Agnes wouldn't have been able to afford to take

A Mother's Love

me in were it not for the monthly checks from my parents' lawyer.

After dinner, Aunt Agnes had me carry some of the leftover food out to the hog pen. I added feed from a barrel in the shed to the leftovers and filled the water trough. Then, I returned to the house and joined the others in front of the TV. By nine o'clock, the difference in time zones had caught up with me. I yawned, and Aunt Agnes immediately got up and went to the kitchen. A few minutes later, she came back with a tray holding five cups.

"We always have hot chocolate at bedtime," she explained. "It's another one of our family traditions." She passed out the cups, and I noticed they had names on them. "We have our names on the cups. I'll order one for you, but in the meantime, you can use your uncle's old cup."

Having personal cups was a bit strange, but then again, I was an only child. I supposed it avoided unnecessary arguments over whose cup was whose.

After saying goodnight to my aunt, I followed my cousins up the creaky stairs. We lined up to use the bathroom. When it was my turn, I brushed my teeth before returning to my bedroom, turning out the light, and crawling into bed. Pale moonlight streamed in through the window, dimly illuminating the unfamiliar room. Despite the strange bed, I fell asleep almost immediately.

Sometime later, the creaking of Aunt Agnes coming up the stairs woke me. She surprised me

A Cauldron of Uncanny Dreams

when she paused outside my door instead of continuing to her bedroom. I wondered if she was going to look in to check if I was okay, but I heard the door opposite mine opening and then closing. Apparently, Aunt Agnes had entered Anna's room. Curious, I listened until Anna's door opened some ten minutes later, and the footsteps continued down the hall to Aunt Agnes' bedroom. Since I had not heard my aunt and Anna talking, I couldn't help wondering what my aunt was doing in Anna's bedroom while she slept.

The next morning, Colin knocked on my door, waking me from a dreamless sleep. "Time to get up, Ethan. Mom said you need to come down if you want breakfast before you start on your chores."

I got up, put on clean clothes, and headed downstairs.

Once again, Aunt Agnes had loaded the dining room table with food, including bacon, eggs, hash browns, and pancakes. Everything tasted wonderful, and I found myself again eating more than I should have. It was clear I'd need to do a lot of hiking and chores if I didn't want to end up as chubby as my cousins. As she had done during dinner, my aunt restricted herself to a bowl of chicken broth and a glass of pulpless orange juice.

After breakfast, I helped Aunt Agnes clear the table and do the dishes. Then she sent me outside to feed the hog and collect eggs from the chicken coop. Once I was done, my aunt said I could do whatever I wanted until lunchtime.

A Mother's Love

"Did my uncle ever go fishing?" I asked. "I was wondering if he had a fishing rod I could use."

"My Frank loved to fish before he got sick," Aunt Agnes said. "I'm sure his old rod and tackle box are around here somewhere. Check out in the shed. If they're not there, you can look up in the attic. It should be in one of those places. If not, I might have gotten rid of it, but I'll buy you a new one if I need to. It would be nice to have some fresh fish again."

While I still really missed my mom and dad, I began to feel like I was part of the family. I helped with the heavy chores that were hard for Aunt Agnes to do. And in the fall, my aunt began homeschooling us. We fell into a comfortable routine.

But in October, I noticed I began to get tired easily and often got out of breath when I occasionally hiked in the woods above our house. I also started having episodes when I seemed paler than normal. I began to worry that I might be catching what my cousins had, but Aunt Agnes said I probably just needed to spend more time doing things outdoors. Since my skin didn't show any signs of being sensitive to sunlight, I guessed she was probably right and promised myself to go hiking more often.

Then, as the weeks passed, I started having a reoccurring nightmare. I'd dream that a monster lurked in the dark corner of my bedroom opposite my bed. The creature glared hungrily at me from the shadows, and I couldn't help but stare back at it. However, it was cloaked in darkness, and I could never see it clearly. All I could tell was that it was roughly the shape and size of a person. Naturally, when the dream woke me, I'd glance over at the corner, but it was always empty.

Eventually, my nightmares turned into night terrors. The monster would leave its dark corner to creep closer to my bed. I wanted to get up and run for the door, but I was paralyzed! Each night, the monster inched closer until it eventually sat down on the bed next to me. It leaned over me and placed a bony hand on my chest. The hand was so heavy I could hardly breathe and felt as though I were suffocating. I tried to cry out and scream for help, but I could neither open my mouth nor make the slightest noise. Yet even though the monster's face was so close to mine that I could feel its warm breath, I still couldn't see it clearly. And when the night terror eventually ended, and I could move again, I was alone in my room.

I tried to ignore my dreams, for I was sure that was all they were. I briefly considered locking my door and then even blocking it by leaning a chair under its doorknob. But I knew I was only having nightmares, and no matter how real they seemed, they couldn't hurt me. I was too old to let myself be terrified by dreams. Eventually, I decided my dreams were merely my mind's way of trying to deal with the death of my parents. I was sure that sooner or later, I would come to terms with my loss, and the nightmares would cease.

A Mother's Love

Then, late one November night while everyone else was asleep, I woke from my reoccurring nightmare. I tried to go back to sleep, but scenes from the dream kept replaying in my mind, and sleep wouldn't come. It didn't help that I was also hungry. Normally, I'd have eaten something from my stash of candy and junk food that I'd bought down at the camp store. But I'd already eaten everything in the box I kept hidden on the back of the shelf in my closet. After half an hour of tossing and turning, I decided I had to head down to the kitchen for a late-night snack.

It was well past two in the morning. With everyone sound asleep, nothing disturbed the silent darkness. Using my phone's flashlight app, I crept quietly down the hallway. Going down the stairs, I carefully avoided stepping on the two steps I knew would creak loudly.

The kitchen floor was cold, and I silently cursed myself for forgetting to wear my slippers. I checked the refrigerator, which always contained the previous day's leftovers that I hadn't given to the hog. But nothing looked all that appetizing, and I certainly didn't want to have to heat any of the cold food on the stove. Not for the first time, I wondered why my aunt had never bought a microwave.

Aunt Agnes didn't like to keep junk food because she felt it wasn't healthy. Still, I wondered whether she might have kept some hidden for special occasions. I didn't find anything in the pantry, so I took a chair from the kitchen table and began methodically working my way around the kitchen cabinets.

I had searched nearly all of them and was beginning to resign myself to eating some cold left-over fried chicken. That's when I spotted an unlabeled box hiding behind a stack of seldom used mixing bowls. It was exactly the kind of place I'd have chosen to hide junk food from a house full of hungry kids. I set the box on the table and opened it.

But the box didn't hold snacks. Instead, it was filled with dozens upon dozens of pill bottles! I read the labels and discovered they all contained the same medicine, one that I'd never heard of before. I also noticed the pill bottles had come from different pharmacies. That didn't make any sense until I realized my aunt might have done it to prevent the pharmacists from questioning why she needed so much of the same medicine. Finally, I discovered a pad of blank prescription forms and realized my aunt was illegally forging the prescriptions.

Was Aunt Agnes secretly addicted to prescription painkillers? Was that why she was willing to break the law to get so many pills?

Still, something didn't add up. My aunt didn't act like any drug addict I'd ever seen played on TV. I didn't recognize the name of the medicine. So, I wouldn't know for sure until I googled it and learned whether it was actually an opioid painkiller.

A Mother's Love

I used my phone's browser to look up the medicine. It wasn't an addictive pain medicine. It was a strong sedative for treating people with severe insomnia! That made no sense. I'd never known my aunt to have insomnia, and besides, why would she need that many pills?

Then, I remembered how I'd get super sleepy every Thursday night after drinking my bedtime hot chocolate. That's when I realized Aunt Agnes must have been drugging me every Thursday for at least the last couple of months! But why would she need so many pills if I was the only one she was drugging? I checked the labels on the pill bottles, and many were dated months before I'd moved in. That meant the pills couldn't have been just for me.

She must have been drugging Connor, Anna, and Jonathon, too! Suddenly, the family tradition of each of us having our name on our mug made sense. She needed the cups labeled, so she could be sure who got the drugged hot chocolate. But why? It still made no sense.

Then, I recalled the times I'd heard her quietly entering my cousins' bedrooms late at night after everyone should have been asleep. Oh my god! She didn't just want us to be asleep, so she could do something without us knowing about it. She wanted us asleep, so she could do something *to us* while we slept! And the only thing I could think of was far too sick and disgusting to consider.

My first thought was to confront her and demand she explain why she was drugging us. But

A Cauldron of Uncanny Dreams

that could be dangerous. Anyone who'd drug her own children was someone who might be capable of anything to keep people from learning her secret. She might even be willing to commit murder. Would she murder me if she learned what I had discovered? I couldn't be sure, and I certainly didn't feel safe.

I quickly loaded the blank prescription pad and pill bottles back into the box. Then I returned it to its hiding place behind the mixing bowls and the chair back at the kitchen table. I looked around the room for any sign that I had been there and sighed with relief when I didn't see any.

My next thought was to call the police. But would they believe me? I had no real evidence. Since the pills weren't prescription narcotics, they couldn't arrest Aunt Agnes for drug dealing. She could just say that she had terrible insomnia, and the pills were only for her.

Perhaps I was wrong. Maybe she had a rational reason for having so many pills, and I was jumping to a terrible, but mistaken, conclusion. If I was wrong, she could lose custody of my cousins and me. I had to be absolutely sure before I called the police.

I realized I only had one choice. In a few hours, it would be Wednesday morning and time to get up. That meant I had only one more night to learn the truth before it would be my turn to get the drugged hot chocolate. Tonight, I'd have to stay awake and wait until I heard her enter one of my cousins' bedrooms. Then, I'd silently creep out

A Mother's Love

and carefully open my cousin's bedroom door just enough so I could peer in. I'd discover what she did in our rooms and use my phone to make a video I could use as evidence. Only then would I know for sure and have the proof I needed.

The next morning when I went down for breakfast, I did my best to act normal despite having discovered Aunt Agnes's stash of pills. I caught myself frequently glancing at her, looking for any sign that she was capable of what I suspected. But I didn't see anything out of the ordinary. In fact, her actions and words only seemed to show her love for her children and me. How could she be drugging us? And yet, I had seen the pills, felt so strangely sleepy after drinking the hot cocoa, and heard her enter my cousins' rooms while they slept. The rest of the day, an uncanny idea wouldn't leave me alone. It was as if two completely different people shared the same body: the Aunt Agnes of the day and the Aunt Agnes of the night.

Eventually, evening came, and Aunt Agnes brought us our nightly mugs of hot chocolate. I had no idea which of my cousins would receive the drugged drink. All I knew was that I was unnaturally sleepy on Thursday nights.

We finished our cocoa, brushed our teeth, and climbed into bed. And then I waited, listening for the sound of my aunt climbing up the stairs.

Eventually, I heard the creaking of the stairs' two loose boards, followed by the soft sound of my aunt's footsteps outside my bedroom. A faint line of candlelight briefly lit the space under my door before dimming as she passed by. Although I dreaded what I might learn, I had to overcome my fear. Silently getting out of bed, I crept to my bedroom door, opened it a crack, and peered out.

Aunt Agnes was standing outside Jonathon's bedroom door, listening. Then, apparently satisfied he was asleep, she slowly opened it, stepped inside, and quietly closed the door behind her.

As stealthily as a cat prowling for mice, I silently crept down the hallway until I stood outside Jonathon's bedroom. I placed my ear on the door and listened. The room was utterly silent. I peered through the keyhole, but all I could see was the foot of his bed. With my hand on the doorknob, I paused, torn between turning it and fleeing back to the safety of my room. At last, I took a deep breath and slowly turned the knob. I opened the door no more than an inch and looked in.

Aunt Agnes was sitting on the bed next to Jonathon. She was leaning over him and holding his bare arm up to her face with her mouth pressed against the inside of his elbow. She paused briefly, lifted her head, and smiled, her expression that of a drug addict getting a fix. A thin trickle of blood welled up and began to dribble down Jonathon's arm. Before it could drip onto his bedcovers, she quickly leaned down and licked the blood from his skin. Then she pressed her mouth

A Mother's Love

to his arm and continued to feed on her youngest son's blood.

Unable to stop myself, I gasped. Aunt Agnes instantly turned around and stared at me with an expression of shock that must have rivaled my own. I did the only things I could. I panicked and ran. I practically flew down the stairs and flung open the front door.

I'd intended to run down to the trailer park and find someone who would let me in and call the police. But I hadn't counted on two inches of blowing snow covering the ground. That's when I realized I was barefoot and wearing thin pajamas that would do nothing to protect me from the icy wind. My shoes and coat were up in my bedroom, and I couldn't go back there.

Since I couldn't leave, I needed a weapon. I raced to the kitchen, grabbed my aunt's biggest butcher's knife, and waited.

I didn't have to wait long. I heard the creaking of my aunt's footsteps on the stairs. Then she stepped into the room and sat down at the kitchen table opposite me.

"You're... you're a vampire!" I knew I was stating the obvious. I knew what I saw, and there was no way she had a perfectly rational explanation for what she was doing in Jonathon's room.

Aunt Agnes sighed with resignation. "Yes, Ethan. I wish to God I wasn't, but I am. And so was my husband until he took the easy way out and killed himself."

"But how could you do this?" I cried. "How can you feed on your own children?"

"I'm doing this for my children!" Aunt Agnes exclaimed. "If I don't have blood, I'll starve. And my children need me! With their father dead, who's going to take care of them if not me? No one's going to adopt three sick children who can't even go outside. I'm all they have."

"But what about the broth? What about the coffee, tea, and soft drinks I've seen you drink at meals?"

"My body can't digest them, and I only drink them to keep hydrated. I can't survive without blood."

My cousins weren't her only victims. I thought of the Friday mornings when I had woken up with unexplained bruises on the inside of one of my elbows. "You haven't just been feeding off my cousins. You've been drinking my blood, too!" I exclaimed as I stared at her in horror.

"I'm sorry, Ethan, but yes. I also feed on your blood. Initially, I tried not to, but I've been taking your blood once a week for several months now. Feeding off you and my friend Clair has enabled me to minimize the blood I'm forced to take from my children."

"Wait. You're saying you actually feed off someone besides us kids? But how?"

A Mother's Love

"Clair and I've been friends since high school. She's the woman down at the mobile home park that I play cards with every Saturday night. It's not that difficult for me to slip something into her tea. And I've had a copy of her house key made, so all I have to do is wait until she's sound asleep and then slip back inside."

I shook my head and thought, *this just keeps getting worse and worse.* "Is there anyone else I should know about?"

"No. Just the hog, though its blood tastes terrible and provides very little nourishment. Once a week, I slip a couple of sleeping pills into the leftovers you take out to him after dinner."

Oh, great, I thought. She's given me the job of drugging the hog. I wasn't just a victim; she made me a party to her animal abuse.

"If I didn't take blood from all of you," she continued, "my hunger might have made me accidentally take too much from my children and kill one of them. Don't you see? I've had no choice."

I'd been grateful to my aunt for giving me a place to live after my parents died. I had trusted her. Hell, I had even begun to love her! But how could she drug me and drink my blood while I slept? Then, the ramification of her feeding on me struck me. "Does that mean that I'm going to turn into a vampire, too? What about my cousins and your friend down at the mobile home park? Oh my God, what about the hog? Are you turning all of us into vampires?"

"No, Ethan. The only way I could turn you into a vampire would be for us to mix our blood together. For example, we'd have to press open wounds together. It can't pass from my saliva into your blood. Besides, I would *never* doom anyone else to the cursed life I live. Never!"

I breathed a huge sigh of relief. The situation was terrible, but it could have been so much worse.

Aunt Agnes tilted her head to the side and looked at me. "So, now that you know my secret, what are you going to do? If you go to the police, they won't believe you. And even if they did, they'd lock me up, and I'd starve to death. You would make my children orphans and all four of you would end up in foster care. Is that really what you want?"

I didn't know what I wanted. Aunt Agnes had admitted what she was and what she had done when she could have lied. She hadn't attacked me and was being truthful. And I was curious. "How did you and my uncle become vampires?"

"I suppose the way all vampires are made," she said with a shrug. "A vampire turned us. One summer, a stranger arrived. His name was Damian. He was traveling by himself, and I suppose he could have been lonely for others of his kind. Anyway, he started by feeding on the people staying down at the camp. But then, he learned that Henry and I were living up here, away from everyone else.

A Mother's Love

Late one night after the children were asleep, he knocked on our door. He had a gun and forced us to swallow some pills that put us to sleep. Once we were unconscious, he fed on us and then rubbed some of his blood into our wounds. The next morning, we found his note telling us he'd kill our children if we told anyone what he'd done. We checked on the children, but they were okay. He hadn't done anything to them, so we figured he'd just drugged us so he could take his time robbing us. When we didn't find anything missing, we assumed he hadn't stolen anything and that we'd been lucky. But we were wrong. All Damian had to do was wait a couple of days for our transition to begin.

"Our first sign of the change was that we became violently sick to our stomachs every time we ate something. We couldn't keep anything down, and despite our nausea, we got hungrier every day. At first, we thought we'd merely eaten something that had gone bad. We decided to see a doctor, but by then, we were too sick and weak to drive.

"That night after we'd put the kids to bed, Damian returned. This time, he knocked on our front door, and we let him in when he said he knew what was wrong with us. Naturally, we didn't believe him when he told us what he'd done. We thought he was crazy and ordered him to get out of our house. But instead of leaving, he opened a satchel he was carrying and took out a mason jar full of a dark red liquid. It was blood, and as soon

A Cauldron of Uncanny Dreams

as we saw it, we were instantly ravenous. He took a drink and then offered it to us. Despite our revulsion, we couldn't help ourselves. Henry drank half, and his nausea instantly vanished. I could see his health and strength returning. He held out the jar to me, and I practically yanked it out of his hand. I drank the rest of the blood, and the experience was overwhelming. It had an intensity like what I imagine a religious ecstasy must be like. It was like drinking the nectar of the gods mixed with water from the fountain of youth. My sickness was gone, and I'd never felt more alive."

Aunt Agnes paused, closing her eyes. A faint smile briefly raised the corners of her mouth before she sighed, and her expression was once again somber. "After that, no doubt remained. Henry and I knew deep in our bones that Damian had told us the truth. We were vampires. But we were also incredibly ignorant and misled by the half-truths and fabrications of vampire books and movies. Damian spent the next hour setting us straight on the basics of what it meant to be a vampire. But then, he said he had some business he had to take care of and would return the following evening to continue our instruction.

"He left us with a thousand and one unanswered questions. We didn't understand what our transformation meant for us and especially what it meant for our children. We talked until dawn. Then, we woke up the kids and tried our best to act as though nothing had happened, and it was just a normal day like any other.

A Mother's Love

"Later that afternoon, Henry drove down to the camp store to pick up some groceries. That's where he learned that Sam Higgins, one of the camp's year-long residents, had shot and killed a stranger who'd tried to break into his trailer in the middle of the night. The stranger's description made it clear that Damian was the man who'd been killed. Everyone assumed the man had intended to rob Sam, but Henry and I knew Damian wasn't after money. He was hunting for blood."

"So, shooting a vampire can kill it?" I asked. "I thought you needed to stake it through the heart."

"Ethan, Damian was a 'him,' not an 'it.' And I'm not one either. Also, the thing about using a stake is mostly a myth. Of course, a stake in the heart will kill anybody. Regardless, Damian died before he could tell us more than the basics about being a vampire. That's also why we never found out why he decided to turn Henry and me instead of someone else."

"So, what did you do then?" I asked.

"We looked up everything we could about vampires," she said. "But we didn't know what to believe and what was mere speculation and fantasy. The only thing we learned for sure was that half of a mason jar of blood only satisfied our hunger for a day. By the third day, we were ravenous and had to get more. I argued that if we only took a little, it would be like someone donating blood. It wouldn't hurt the person. But Henry adamantly argued that we had no right to take anyone's blood. He felt it would be evil. That we were cursed and destined to become evil ourselves.

"I told him I would get us blood from the hog. That way, we wouldn't be hurting anybody. I went out to the hog pen with a large pitcher. I had to kill the animal to get it, but I didn't see how I'd had any other choice. But it tasted terrible and only partially satisfied my hunger. Still, it was better than nothing and lasted us four days."

"Then what did you do? Did you have another hog?"

Aunt Agnes sighed. "No. But I did manage to find a butcher who would sell us ten gallons of cow's blood. He gave me a funny look when I told him I needed it for making blood sausage but was happy enough to take my money and not ask any more questions. That lasted us well over two months, but what our bodies really needed was human blood. By then, we'd lost a lot of weight and were constantly nauseous.

"Henry and I eventually drove up to Olympia and robbed a blood bank. We were terrified we'd get caught and arrested, but Ethan, you got to understand. We were desperate. Luck was with us, and we managed to steal their entire inventory and get away before the cops arrived. We must have been four or five blocks from the blood bank when two cop cars raced past us going in the opposite direction with their lights flashing and sirens blaring. If we had taken just a few more minutes, they would have caught us. We had to

A Mother's Love

make the blood last as long as possible, so we restricted ourselves to drinking as little as we could. We were able to make it last over two months before we ran low. But by limiting ourselves, we were always hungry and continued to lose weight.

"We decided that stealing blood from a blood bank was just too risky to try again. That's when I decided we had no choice but to treat our children as blood donors. Henry vehemently disagreed, and we had a huge fight over it. But I didn't see that we had any other choice. I went to our doctor, told him I had terrible insomnia, and got him to prescribe some sleeping pills. I was also able to steal one of his prescription pads so I could get more.

"But when I arrived home, I found Henry in the bathroom. When he didn't answer me, I was terrified that he'd had a heart attack or something. I broke down the door and found him lying naked in the bathtub. He couldn't accept what I was determined to do and had slit his wrists. Still, he loved me and our children. He had bled into my biggest mixing bowl and nearly filled it before he died."

I was horrified, imagining how my uncle did what he could for my aunt even in the middle of committing suicide.

"Ethan, I was devastated, but what else could I do? I made my Henry's blood last as long as I could before starting our ritual of having hot chocolate. And now you know my story. I only hope that you can eventually come to forgive me for what I've done to you. Believe me. If there had been any other way, I would have taken it."

I wasn't sure I could ever forgive her. Her confession about drugging the hot chocolate reminded me I wasn't her only victim. "Do my cousins know?" I asked.

"What I am? And what I do to them? No, and I would like you to keep it that way."

"But they have a right to know what you're doing to them while they sleep."

"They may have the right, but that doesn't mean you have the right to tell them. I'm their mother, and I'm trying to do what's best for them."

I couldn't believe what I was hearing. "What's best for them? Or what's best for you?"

"Think about it, Ethan. Would their knowing help or hurt them? How would it make their lives any better to know that their mother did this to them? How could they ever trust anyone again? And knowing that if I stopped, it would kill me? How could it help them live with the guilt of being responsible for my death? No, Ethan, they're too young, and this is my cross to bear. At least until they're old enough to understand."

"But what if they find out on their own just like I did? Wouldn't it be less traumatic for them to learn the truth from you?"

"Possibly, but that won't happen, at least not unless you tell them."

A Mother's Love

"But I found out," I argued.

She nodded. "You did. But that's only because you're new to our family and still see us with fresh eyes. With them, it's different. I've been doing this ever since they were little. I had just given birth to Jonathon when Damion turned Frank and me. Your cousins are used to our family routine of hot chocolate before bed. As far as they're concerned, being anemic just runs in our family. I've been very careful to not give them any reason to question their lives."

She paused briefly before continuing. "However, I would like to know what gave me away. What did you see that they don't?"

"One night while everyone else was asleep, I woke up hungry," I replied. "I went down to the kitchen, but since I didn't want to eat cold chicken, I decided to search the cabinets for some junk food. I found your huge stash of prescription sleeping pills. That's when I remembered how sleepy I'd get every Thursday night, and I realized you were drugging me. It didn't take a genius to figure out I wasn't your only victim. You also must have been drugging Connor, Anna, and Jonathon too. That's why you needed so many pills."

Aunt Agnes nodded. "That was clever of you to work that all out on your own. I had to ensure I gave each of you as much time between feedings as I could to keep you from getting too anemic and prevent you from getting addicted to the medicine. I took as little blood as I could as seldom as I could and still function as their mother. That's why I always feel like I'm starving." She looked down at her arms. "It's also why I'm nothing but skin and bones."

"When I found the pills," I continued, "I didn't understand why you needed each of us to be asleep one night a week. Then, I remembered how I'd occasionally hear you entering one of my cousins' bedrooms after we were all supposed to be asleep for the night. That's when I decided to find out what you were doing inside our rooms when you'd drugged us. Now I know. You weren't just using the drug to ensure we were asleep. You were using it to make sure the pain of your bite wouldn't wake us up."

"Yes, Ethan. You figured it all out. And now you know another reason why it was important for me to have you come live with us. Having one more blood donor meant my children could have more time between feedings. But now that you know my secret, I won't be able to take any more of your blood, and I'll have to go back to feeding on your cousins and my friend down at the trailer park more often."

Her quick willingness to give up on taking my blood sent a shiver up my spine. "Since you aren't going to be drugging me anymore to steal my blood, does that mean you're going to kill me to keep me silent?"

"Ethan, I may be desperate, but I'm not a monster. You're just as much a member of our family as my children. You may not believe me, but since I've come to know you, I've also come

A Mother's Love

to love you. So now you know I won't force you to help me, and I certainly wouldn't dream of killing you."

"So, what happens next?" I asked warily.

"You put down that knife, and we both go back to bed," she said. "But I beg you, please don't tell your cousins. And please think about everything I've told you and don't do anything we'll both regret." She sighed. "But if you do decide you have to let them know I'm a vampire, please come to me first. Let me be the one to tell them."

And with that, Aunt Agnes got up and left the kitchen.

I heard the stairs creak and then only silence. I stood there for a few more minutes, unsure of what to do. Then, I sighed, put the butcher knife back in the knife holder, and also went back upstairs to bed. I lay there for at least an hour, obsessing over what I'd seen and everything Aunt Agnes had said, all while listening for any sound outside my door. But eventually, I fell into a mercifully dreamless sleep.

The next morning, Aunt Agnes woke us up, and my cousins and I went down to breakfast. Remembering what I had seen my aunt doing in his room, I couldn't help staring at Jonathon. I couldn't decide whether he was actually a little paler than he had been the previous day, or if it was merely my imagination.

Eventually, Jonathon noticed. "Why do you keep looking at me? Do I have food caught between my teeth or something?"

"No," I said. "It's nothing. I was just thinking." Then I realized that Aunt Agnes was staring at me with a concerned look. I shrugged my shoulders, and we continued having breakfast as though nothing out of the ordinary had happened.

Several days passed without me being any closer to deciding whether my cousins needed to be told now rather than after they were all adults. So, I decided to put off making the decision. I came to realize that although our family definitely wasn't exactly what anyone would call normal, it was nevertheless functional in its own unique way. As the days passed, we all settled into our routines, and I came to understand that my aunt was doing the best she could in the terrible situation that had been forced on her. I started to empathize with her, pity her, and love her for who, not what, she was.

As days turned into weeks and months, Aunt Agnes and I came to an understanding. I would keep her secrets and not tell anyone what I had learned. And she would tell my cousins everything once Jonathon turned eighteen, and they were all adults. To help prevent Aunt Agnes from taking too much blood from my cousins, I even agreed to let her take a little of mine each week. Since there was no way that I was going to let her feed on me while I slept, I made her use an IV while I was awake. It may have been more painful that way,

A Mother's Love

but it did enable me to consider it as being no different from donating at a blood drive. After all, it was only blood, and it could have been worse. She could have needed a kidney.

Author's Comments

There are countless vampire stories that portray vampires as inherently evil. I thought it would be interesting to write the story of a vampire who is sympathetic despite committing the ordinarily terribly evil act of feeding on her children.

A Cauldron of Uncanny Dreams

THE GOVERNESS

It was a cold October evening as the lamplighter with his ladder slowly worked his way down Wigmore Street. He ignited the gaslights one by one, doing his duty to drive back the deepening gloom. Standing near the top of his ladder, he paid no heed to the passing hansom cabs or the occasional pedestrian walking below him. Similarly, the worthy residents who lived around Portman Square ignored the workman as they hurried home, eager to get inside before the rising fog wrapped London in its cold and wet embrace.

The lamplighter failed to notice the pale woman, who paused to hold a piece of paper up to the light from the streetlamp. Then, having confirmed the address, she silently walked on until she reached her destination: the three-story residence of the widowed merchant, Mr. Marcus Wellington, and his nine-year-old son, David.

The woman lifted the heavy ring of the brass lion-head door knocker and let it fall. The resulting boom reverberated inside the still house, but the thickening shroud of fog outside seemed to smother the sound. When no one answered, she raised her hand once more to the knocker but withdrew it when she heard the door being unlocked. She expected to see a young maid or perhaps even a butler, but it was a rather rotund middle-aged woman who opened the door.

The Governess

"My name is Mrs. Whitehall," the young woman said, holding up the advertisement that had prompted her arrival. "Clara Whitehall. I've come about the governess position for an invalid boy. Is it still available?"

"It is. Come in out of the cold before you catch your death."

Neither tall nor short, Clara Whitehall was a slender woman in her late twenties. Although her modest clothing was a few years out of style, such as what an older woman might wear, it was clean and well cared for.

"I am Mrs. O'Grady, Mr. Wellington's housekeeper. The master is in his study. Wait here, and I shall inform him of your arrival."

Clara looked around the foyer with interest. A large Chinese vase stood on a small table, and a pair of Dutch landscape paintings graced the walls. In the corner, an elephant foot umbrella stand held a silver-handled cane and a black umbrella to protect the master from London's frequent rains.

Mrs. O'Grady soon returned. "The master will see you now. Please follow me." Then the housekeeper turned and led Clara into the study.

Mr. Wellington sat behind a massive oak desk while an old woman dressed all in black stood by the fire. The prosperous merchant studied Clara with undisguised curiosity and more than a bit of surprise. Knowing that she was older than most governesses, Clara assumed her age surprised him.

Meanwhile, the woman in black silently nodded to Clara. She wore a self-satisfied smile, as though taking credit for a meaningful accomplishment.

Mr. Wellington stood and walked around his desk. He circled Clara, examining her as if she were an object that he considered purchasing rather than an honest woman seeking employment. His unexpected behavior made her feel nervous.

Apparently satisfied, he returned to his seat. "Mrs. O'Grady tells me you have come to apply for the governess position. My son David suffers from a severe debility of the lower extremities that keeps him bedridden. What experience do you have caring for invalid children?"

"I took care of my son Charles for nearly three years after the carriage accident that shattered his legs," Clara replied. "He was as healthy and happy as any mother could hope for until the grippe took him. So, I can take good care of your son and am not afraid of the hard work that entails. You'll not find anyone better than me."

"And what of Mr. Whitehall and any other children you might have? This position requires your presence both day and night, should my son have need of you."

"The illness that took our only son also took my husband. I am thus alone and free from all commitments."

Mr. Wellington turned to the older woman by the fire. "And what say you, Mrs. Black? You are the expert in these matters."

The Governess

"She answered my call. She is the one that David needs."

The old woman's words confused Clara, but she desperately needed the position. Without her husband's income and with her meager savings all but gone, she could not pay the rent on her small flat, and the landlord threatened to put her out on the street. As a governess, she would undoubtedly have a room in the servants' quarters and thus have no need to pay for lodging.

Mr. Wellington turned back to Clara. "My business frequently takes me away from London, often for weeks at a time. Until last summer when my poor wife passed from consumption, I relied on her to care for David in my absence. I am afraid that since then, he has been inconsolable and suffers greatly from a deep melancholy. In my absence, I must rely on you to teach him reading, writing, and arithmetic. More importantly, you will keep him company and cure his loneliness. Since his mother's death, he often wakes from nightmares so terrible that his piteous cries disturb the entire household. At such times, I will expect you to hold his hand until he returns to sleep."

Clara looked back at Mr. Wellington with sympathy and concern. "My son Charles often had such nightmares, and the pain in his legs often woke him. I would hold his hand until the laudanum eased his suffering. I will care for your David as I cared for my own son." Clara paused briefly. "Now that my husband has passed, I must both support myself and save for an old age free from poverty. What remuneration might I expect?"

Mr. Wellington paused only briefly before answering. "Besides room and board, I will pay you five shillings a week."

Mr. Wellington's great generosity surprised Clara, for a full pound every month was far more than she expected. A position of importance in a fine house offered her a secure future, at least until David was no longer a child. Her position would do more than save her from a miserable life in the workhouse or some squalid tenement. It would even enable her to save several shillings each month.

"I gratefully accept your kind offer."

"Then Mrs. O'Grady will see you to your room," Mr. Wellington said. "I have pressing business in Brussels and must leave on the morning train to Dover. I shall be gone for a fortnight. In my absence, rely on Mrs. O'Grady. She will acquaint you with the rules of the house and report to me on my son's progress." He stood and pulled one of several cords that hung from the wall behind his desk, and a bell rang in the hallway.

Mrs. O'Grady appeared shortly thereafter. "Yes, Mr. Wellington?"

"Mrs. Whitehall will be David's governess and will report to you while I am away. Please show her to her room."

The Governess

"Yes, Mr. Wellington," Mrs. O'Grady replied. "Please follow me, Mrs. Whitehall." Then she turned and led Clara out of the study.

Once the two had left, and Mrs. O'Grady had closed the door behind them, Mr. Wellington turned to the old woman standing by the fire. "Mrs. Black, are you certain she is what you promised? I must say, she seems to be no more nor no less than what she appears to be."

"I am quite certain, Mr. Wellington. Her silver aura is as clear to me as any I have ever seen. She is precisely what I promised."

"But she seems to be totally unaware of her situation. How is that possible?"

"Losing her husband and her son has burned a hole in Clara Whitehall's soul. She will find no peace until she fills that hole with the love of another child. Your child, Mr. Wellington. It is the same injury the loss of his mother has caused your son. They will heal each other."

Mr. Wellington nodded. "Mrs. Black. You said you would find an appropriate governess, and it seems that you have. Despite your many references, I couldn't quite believe you could find so suitable a solution." He reached into the breast pocket of his suit, removed a leather wallet, and pulled out several large banknotes. "As agreed, here are the initial fifty pounds that I promised you. If on my return, she has eased my son's suffering and removed the cloud of melancholy enveloping this house, I shall pay you the remaining two-hundred-and-fifty pounds."

Mrs. Black took the banknotes, folded them, and placed them safely in her purse. Soon, she would add another ten pounds from Clara's landlord. Hearing her frequent crying through the building's thin walls had unnerved his other tenants, who had begun to demand her removal. "Do not worry, Mr. Wellington. Clara Whitehall is just what your son needs to help him cope with the loss of his dear mother."

"I know it is quite late, but might I look in on the boy?" Clara asked as Mrs. O'Grady led Clara up the stairs towards her new room in the third-floor servant quarters. "I promise not to wake him."

"I suppose it will be all right," she answered hesitantly. "But first, what did the master tell you of his son?"

"Only that the young boy suffers from a severe debility of his lower extremities that keeps him bedridden. That and he suffers from a deep melancholy since the passing of his mother."

"Did the master make no mention of anything else?"

"Just that the boy also suffers from terrible nightmares, and his crying wakens him and the staff. Why do you ask?"

"Well, if that is all the master has said, then far be it from me to say more. Besides, you shall learn the truth soon enough."

The Governess

Mrs. O'Grady led Clara to a closed door on the second floor. "This... this is the young master's room," the housekeeper said. "See for yourself."

Clara gingerly opened the door a few inches and peered into the darkened room. At first, it appeared empty, but she soon noticed the small figure lying peacefully and still beneath the bed's comforter. Then she carefully closed the door. "The poor little boy. He looks no bigger than my poor Charles before the grippe took him."

Mrs. O'Grady looked at Clara and crossed herself.

"That a child at such a tender age should suffer so from the loss of his mother must weigh heavily on the master," Clara continued.

"I'll show you to your room," Mrs. O'Grady said, as she led Clara up to the third floor where the servants lived. She opened the door to an empty room. It was quite small, just large enough for a bed, a wardrobe, a chest of drawers, and a small writing table. Clara would return to her modest apartment in the morning and gather up the few clothes and mementos that she would keep. The rest of their unneeded possessions she would leave behind for the next renters to use or sell as they saw fit. Clara said goodnight to the housekeeper, lay down on the bed, and closed her eyes.

Just after midnight, a young boy's screams of terror roused Clara from a deep and dreamless sleep. His heartbroken cries continued as he called for his mother. Clara rapidly lit a candle and descended the narrow servants' stairway to where Mr. Wellington, Mrs. O'Grady, and one of the maids had gathered outside the little boy's room.

"Let me through," Clara said as she swept past them and into the room. She placed the candleholder on the nightstand and sat down on the bed next to the master's young son. Although still asleep, David violently thrashed about as though fighting the demons of Hell itself. "Wake up, David," she said as she gently shook the boy's shoulders. "'Tis only a dream. Just a bad dream and nothing more."

The boy opened his eyes. "Mamma?" he asked, looking up in confusion.

"No, David. Your mother is with the angels. My name is Clara, and I am your new governess."

"You're not mamma?"

"No, little one," Clara said, taking David's small hand in her own. "Your dear mamma sent me to look after you. You're safe now. I'll protect you from the terrors of the night."

David looked around the room, and seeing no monsters, he began to relax. "Will you stay with me?" he asked, wiping the tears from his eyes.

"Of course, I will, dear child," Clara said, tenderly brushing the hair back from his eyes. "I'll stay right here holding your hand till you fall asleep. And then I'll stay a little while longer so that you needn't have any fear. Tomorrow morning, we can get to know each other. Does that sound good?"

The Governess

David nodded and closed his eyes.

Clara glanced back at Mr. Wellington, who was standing silently in the doorway.

"Thank you," he whispered before closing the door.

Over the following weeks, if one were to stand outside David's room and place their ear on the door, they could hear the soft sounds of Clara's and David's voices. During the day, they would hear Clara teaching the young boy reading, writing, and arithmetic. And in the evenings, they would hear her reading aloud the latest novels of H. G. Wells, Jules Verne, Mark Twain, and Robert Louis Stevenson.

As time passed, a bond formed between the governess and the little boy as each came to fill the hole in the other's heart. David's nightmares grew less frequent, and the house eventually remained still and peaceful from dusk to dawn. The voices coming from the boy's room grew fainter until one day, they could be heard no more.

The dark cloud of melancholy had finally lifted from the Wellington residence. The grateful merchant happily paid Mrs. Black the remaining two-hundred and fifty pounds, for while the priest's exorcism had failed to end the haunting of Wellington House, the spiritualist had succeeded in enabling the ghosts of both David Wellington and Clara Whitehall to pass on.

Author's Comments

A Cauldron of Uncanny Dreams

I wanted to write a traditional Victorian ghost story. I also like the idea of ghosts being unaware they are ghosts.

HEXENDORF

The young American newlyweds, Bill and Sophie Meyer, were honeymooning in Austria, the country Bill's paternal ancestors emigrated from. They started by staying several days in Vienna, where Bill had been a university student studying European history. Before continuing to Innsbruck, Bill planned to stop at Kleindorf, a small village just east of the Austrian Alps. Kleindorf was the hometown of his great-great-grandfather, Heinrich Meyer. It was also the source of a strange family legend passed down through Heinrich's descendants until Bill eventually heard the story as an impressionable young child.

According to the legend, Heinrich Meyer was in one of his pastures with his milk cows late one April afternoon. He noticed smoke rising from the nearby woods and entered to investigate. He was astounded to find a tiny village of six small houses a mere hundred meters from the edge of his field. Having spent countless hours in those woods as a young boy, Heinrich knew for certain that no such hamlet existed.

Speaking with an unusual accent, the dour inhabitants told Heinrich their village had always been there. Although they urged him to stop by the village gasthaus and sample the local beer, Heinrich had to leave because he needed to return his cows to his barn for milking.

That evening, he told his wife and friends about his strange discovery. The next morning, he led them into the woods, but the mysterious village had vanished. Although Heinrich swore that he had really seen the little hamlet, no one believed his crazy story. And from that day forward, the people of Kleindorf thought something wasn't quite right with him.

Intrigued by the family legend, Bill planned to use his visit to Kleindorf as an opportunity to look for the strange village himself. And although Sophie expected the search to be a waste of time, Bill's heart was set on finding the source of the story. So, she willingly agreed to support him and spend a day looking.

Early on the evening of April 29th, Bill and Sophie arrived in Kleindorf and checked into their room at the *Gasthaus zu Alten Kamoraden*. After unpacking, they went down to the common room where they enjoyed a traditional Austrian dinner of Wiener Schnitzel and apfelstrudel washed down with the local beer. Then they retired early to their room, as newlyweds often do.

The next morning after breakfast, Bill and Sophie visited the local church where the young priest happily helped them locate Bill's ancestors in the baptismal registry. With the priest's help, Bill extended his family tree all the way back to the early 1700s. They also confirmed that the Meyers were dairy farmers before Heinrich emigrated with his family to the United States. Unfortunately, there was no record of to whom Heinrich had sold

Hexendorf

his farm. So, Bill and Sophie did not know where to begin their search for the missing village, only that Heinrich's pastures had to be somewhere within walking distance of his farm.

After lunch, Bill and Sophie set out on their search for the mysterious village. They were able to ignore each of the nearby villages on the main roads because each was well known in Heinrich's time. Instead, the couple looked for a small cluster of old houses or any sign of ruins in nearby woods or farmer's fields. As Sophie expected, they spent the entire afternoon searching the picturesque countryside without success.

"Let's head back to the gasthaus," Sophie said as the afternoon sun dipped toward the distant Alps. "We've been driving these back roads for hours and haven't seen a sign of your great-great-grandfather's lost village. If it ever existed, it's probably long gone after all these years."

"Just another hour, Sophie. I have a hunch we're close. It's got to be around here somewhere. We just haven't driven on the right road yet."

"Thirty minutes, Bill, and then we head back," she answered. "It's dinnertime, and I'm starting to get hungry. We can always look again tomorrow. But first, I want to see if we can print out a Google Maps satellite view of the area. If we're going to spend another day looking for Heinrich's lost village, I want to do a systematic search and mark off each road we go down instead of driving around at random."

They soon came upon an old dirt road that was little more than a pair of ruts worn into the ground. It led across a farmer's field and into the nearby forest.

Bill brought the car to a stop just shy of the turnoff. "Look over there," he said, pointing to where several thin streams of smoke rose into the air. "This could be it."

"Okay," Sophie said. "But if it doesn't pan out, let's call it a day."

They turned off the paved road and followed the narrow lane that led into the woods. A hundred meters later, they reached a clearing in which a small gasthaus and half-a-dozen one-story houses were arranged in a circle. A large pile of firewood dominated the center, while an old-fashioned stone well stood next to the two-story *Gasthaus Hexendorf.* The buildings were of unpainted wood that years of weather had colored gray. Several elderly men and women in traditional Austrian clothing eyed them and their car suspiciously as Bill parked in front of the inn.

"The people here aren't exactly friendly," Sophie observed as she stared back at the grim-faced inhabitants who stood in small groups. They pointed at the car, shook their heads, and spoke in hushed tones.

"They probably don't get many tourists," Bill replied. "Let's go inside. We can have dinner and sample their local beer. After we've eaten, I can ask the proprietor about the history of their village."

Hexendorf

"Okay," Sophie said, as she followed her husband into the inn's dimly lit common room. It was empty except for the old man standing behind the bar.

"*Willkommen im Gasthaus Hexendorf,*" the old man said, speaking in German with an extremely strong Austrian accent. "*Was wünschen die gnädige Herr und Dame?*"

"What did he say?" Sophie asked. The few German phrases Bill had taught her were insufficient, especially given the man's accent.

"Welcome to the Gasthaus Hexendorf," Bill answered. "And then he asked us what we'd like. I'll ask him for the menu and two of his local beers." Turning to the bartender, Bill replied, speaking with the 'accent-free,' high German one heard on TV.

The bartender turned toward the door to the kitchen and shouted, "*Perchta! Wir haben Kunden!*"[1]

A few seconds later, a beautiful young woman with raven-black hair and emerald-green eyes entered the common room. The bartender handed her two large stoneware steins. The waitress placed the tankards of beer on the table, leaning suggestively toward Bill so that her traditional low-cut dirndl dress prominently displayed her ample bosom. Completely ignoring Sophie, Perchta smiled at Bill and said, "*Guten Tag, mein Schatz. Bist du hungrig? Wir haben Jägerschnitzel und geröstete Kartoffeln.*"[2]

---

[1] Perchta, we have customers.

"*Ja, bitte*," Bill answered, ignoring the waitress's use of the endearment, 'my treasure.'

As Perchta headed back to the kitchen, Bill turned to Sophie and translated, "She said hello and asked me if we're hungry. Then she said they're serving *Jägerschnitzel* and roasted potatoes. I told her that would be fine."

"What's *Jägerschnitzel?*" Sophie asked.

"It's a breaded and fried veal cutlet served with mushroom gravy. I think you'll like it. It was one of my favorites when I studied at the University of Vienna."

In a surprisingly short time, Perchta returned with their dinners, once again leaning low in front of Bill, who was beginning to feel uncomfortable. She looked at Bill's beer stein and noticed that he had only finished a little of the full liter of beer she had brought him. "Drink up," she said in German. "I'm sure you must be thirsty."

Bill suddenly realized that he was indeed very thirsty. He took a drink and found that the beer tasted far better than it had just a few minutes earlier.

Meanwhile, Sophie took her first bite of food and frowned. "Bill, what type of mushrooms are these? I don't think I like their flavor. They're too…" She paused for several seconds, trying to think of an appropriate word. "They taste kind of musty."

---

[2] Good day, my treasure. Are you hungry? We have hunter schnitzel and roasted potatoes.

Hexendorf

Ignoring her question, Bill guzzled the rest of his beer. When He put down the empty mug, Perchta stepped up and gave him another.

"Sophie, this beer is amazing!" Bill said.

"Really?" she asked. "I suppose it's okay, but I've certainly had better. It tastes kind of off to me."

"Off?" Bill asked. "I think this might be the best beer I've ever tasted, and I've tried most of the Austrian and German beers when I was at the university." Ignoring his food, he picked up the second beer and drank half of it.

"Bill, maybe you should slow down and have some of your food," Sophie suggested, concerned by his drinking. "These beer steins hold more than a quart."

"Slow down?" Bill asked. "Why should I slow down when the beer is this good?"

"You've hardly touched your food," Sophie answered. "And if you keep drinking like that, you won't be in any shape to drive." What she thought, but didn't say, was that he would also be too drunk when they were finally alone back in their room at the inn.

Perchta brought Bill a new mug of beer each time he finished one, and soon he was obviously drunk. "Excuse me," he said, slurring his words. He stood up and staggered off in search of the gasthaus's restroom.

By that point, Sophie was confused, concerned, and not a little irritated by Bill's behavior.

Sophie was surprised when Bill took longer to return than expected. And when he did reenter the common room, he wasn't alone. Perchta had her arm around his waist and was clearly the only reason he could walk without falling. Worse, his shirt was untucked, its top two buttons were undone, and he had a shit-eating grin plastered on his face.

Perchta dropped Bill onto his chair. She stared at Sophie with a self-satisfied smirk. And then she sat on Bill's lap and wrapped her arms around his shoulders!

"Bill!" Sophie exclaimed as she jumped up. Feeling shocked, betrayed, and furious, she glared at the waitress and shouted, "Get off my husband!" Balling her hands into fists, she wanted nothing more than to slap that smile off the woman's face. "Bill, get up! We're leaving!"

Bill completely ignored her, and Perchta laughed.

"Bill!" Sophie wailed as tears blurred her vision. When Bill showed no sign that he had even heard her, Sophie turned and ran for the door. "Damn that bitch!" she cursed as she stormed out of the gasthaus, slamming the door behind her. Then she climbed into the car and raced out of the little village.

Fifteen minutes later, she was back in Kleindorf, parking in front of the *Gasthaus Zu Alten Kamoraden*. She barged into the common room, marched up to the bartender, and angrily asked, "What do you have that's stronger than beer?"

"We have schnaps," he answered. "What type do you want?"

"I don't care. You pick one."

The bartender selected a bottle of clear liquid and poured some into a shot glass.

Sophie downed the pear schnaps, feeling its warmth travel down to her stomach. "Again"

The bartender refilled her glass. "Are you all right, Frau Meyer?"

Sophie looked at him, doing her best to keep from crying. "No. I'm not."

The bartender looked at her sympathetically and asked, "May I ask what happened?"

"My husband and I drove all over, looking for the mysterious village his great-great-grandfather said appeared and then disappeared. We were almost ready to give up and return here for dinner when we spotted an overgrown dirt road that led across a farmer's field and into a forest. We followed it and came to a tiny village with half-a-dozen decrepit houses and a run-down gasthaus."

"That doesn't sound like any village around here," the bartender observed. "What was the gasthaus called?"

"Gasthaus Hexendorf."

"Are you sure, Frau Meyer? I'm afraid there's no gasthaus with that name anywhere within a hundred kilometers."

"Of course, I'm sure! And it's not more than a fifteen-minute drive from here."

The bartender shook his head. "If you say so, Frau Meyer. And where is Herr Meyer?"

"I left the bastard there. The waitress got him drunk, and she ended up sitting on his lap. He completely ignored me, and if that wasn't bad enough, she laughed at me. Perchta actually laughed at me!"

The bartender's face went white when he heard the name. "Stay right here, Frau Meyer. There's someone you need to talk to. I'll call her. I'm sure she'll want to meet you and come right over." He took out his phone and dialed a number. "*Frau Steiner. Ich bin's, Matthias Schneider. Eine Frau Meyer ist hier mit mir, und sie sagt, dass sie und ihr Mann Perchta gesehen hat! Wo? In Hexendorf! Kommen Sie sofort. Bis bald.*"[3]

The bartender turned back to Sophie and said, "That was Frau Steiner. I told her you've seen Perchta in Hexendorf. She needs to tell you about a similar experience she and her husband had there fifty years ago."

Not five minutes later, an elderly woman entered the gasthaus and walked right up to Sophie. "Have you really been to Hexendorf and seen Perchta?"

---

[3] Frau Steiner. It's me, Matthias Schneider. A Frau Meyer is here with me, and she says that she and her husband have seen Perchta. Where? In Hexendorf. Come immediately. See you soon.

Hexendorf

"Yes," Sophie said. "But she can't be the same woman. She couldn't have been more than twenty-five, and Herr Schneider said you met her fifty years ago."

"Was she beautiful and seductive? Did she have raven hair? Green eyes?"

"Yes, but…"

"Then it was her, Frau Meyer. Perchta is no ordinary woman. She's a witch. Actually, she's a dead witch who is even more powerful now than when she was alive. Several centuries ago, the villagers burned her at the stake, but before they lit the fire, she cursed them. She renamed the village *Hexendorf*, which means Witch Village in English. Perchta told the villagers that within a week, they would all be dead. She said their village would vanish, only to reappear for a single night once every fifty years. On this very night, Frau Meyer. We call April 30th *Hexennacht* or witches' night. So, if you're telling the truth, Perchta and Hexendorf have returned."

"But that's crazy," Sophie argued.

"No, Frau Meyer. It may be hard to believe, but it is true, nonetheless. I lost my dear husband Heinrich to Perchta exactly fifty years ago."

"Lost?" Sophie asked. "What do you mean, lost?"

"When Hexendorf vanished, so did Heinrich. I never saw him again. Where is your husband, Frau Meyer?"

A Cauldron of Uncanny Dreams

"Oh, no!" Sophie exclaimed. "When Perchta sat on his lap, and he ignored me, I left him with her in Hexendorf!"

"You must not blame your husband," Frau Steiner said, taking Sophie's hand in hers. "Perchta has bewitched him. And if you don't rescue him and leave before sunrise, he will never leave Hexendorf. Perchta will burn him alive, just like the villagers burned her. She will doom him to join the ghosts of those she has killed, and he will haunt Hexendorf forever."

"But if Perchta is so powerful, what chance do I have against her?"

"It is a slim chance," Frau Steiner admitted. "But if you love your husband, you have no choice but to take it."

"What must I do?" Sophie asked.

"Are you wearing your crucifix?"

"No," Sophie answered. "I'm not catholic. Why do you ask?"

"Frau Meyer, I ask because it is vital. Perchta had no trouble casting spells on my husband, but when she tried to cast one on me, nothing happened. That's when she noticed my crucifix and cursed me for wearing it. My crucifix saved my life fifty years ago. If only my poor Heinrich had worn his, we both might have escaped Hexendorf."

"But I'm not religious. Will a crucifix still work for me?"

Hexendorf

"It is enough that Perchta fears them. We must go to the church and get two crucifixes, one for you to wear and one for your husband."

"But what about the villagers? Won't she just order them to capture us and physically prevent us from leaving before sunrise?"

"You are right to worry for that is what she did fifty years ago to Heinrich and me. Two of them held Heinrich, and my crucifix did not stop several of them from trying to grab me. Thank God, I was a very fast runner fifty years ago. How fast are you?"

"I don't know. I've never been chased by ghosts before. If the crucifixes don't stop the villagers, what can I use instead?"

"I'm not sure," Frau Steiner replied. "Perhaps holy water. Maybe throwing holy water can keep them away from you long enough to escape." Frau Steiner glanced up at the cuckoo clock on the wall above the bar. "It will be midnight in half an hour. We must hurry. I fear that she might sacrifice your husband at midnight."

Frau Steiner quickly led Sophie to the village's little Catholic church where they found two crucifixes. Sophie put one of them around her neck, being careful to ensure it was visible over her blouse. They also found a bottle of communion wine. After emptying it, Sophie refilled it with holy water from the bronze font on the wall by the front door.

"Go now, Frau Meyer. Hurry. You must get to your husband before Perchta burns him alive. Good luck and may the Blessed Virgin Mary watch over you."

Thus, armed for battle, Sophie jumped into her car and raced along the road leading back to Hexendorf and her husband.

...

Meanwhile, in Hexendorf, Perchta's magic had Bill totally under her spell. He knew only that she enthralled him. His eyes only saw her beauty, and his ears only heard her seductively appealing voice. He did not hear the ticking of the antique wooden cuckoo clock hanging on the wall behind the bar. He did not hear it growing steadily louder as the final few minutes before midnight passed.

Perchta and the bartender stared intently at the clock, watching the minute hand slowly approach the hour hand. With a final tick, they both pointed straight up at the roman numeral XII. A little bird popped out, and twelve times, it sang, cuckoo. Midnight had arrived.

Perchta leaped up from Bill's lap and cried, "*Mitternacht!*"[4] Then she laughed, but her pleasant voice was cold and hard as her laughter became a malevolent cackle.

Bill looked directly at Perchta, but he couldn't see that her youth and voluptuous beauty had vanished, leaving her an ancient hideous hag with

---

[4] Midnight!

Hexendorf

sparse, stringy gray hair on an age-spotted scalp, a hooked nose, and milky white eyes. A long black dress marred by rips and burn marks had replaced her traditional, low-cut dirndl dress. Bill only saw what the witch wanted him to see.

"*Komm mit mir, Liebchen!*"[5] she commanded, grabbing one of his hands with gnarled bony fingers. She effortlessly pulled him up from his chair and led him out into the cold dark night. "*Wir müssen das Lagerfeuer anzünden und tanzen!*"[6] she said in her heavily accented German. Pointing a long and crooked finger at the large pile of firewood piled up in the open area in front of the gasthaus, Perchta yelled, "*Feuer!*"

Fire sprang up, instantly engulfing the woodpile and sending flames, sparks, and dense black smoke into the cloudy sky. Earlier, the old wooden homes and gasthaus had merely appeared gray with age. But now, the buildings were dark and decrepit, with empty windows, leaning walls, and caved-in roofs that lay open to the night.

The villagers had also changed. Their bodies were ravaged by decay, and they wore bits and tatters of rotted clothing. Those lost souls started to shuffle around the bonfire, chanting, "Perchta! Perchta! Perchta!" They began to dance the terrible Totentanz, the hellish Dance of Death.

Perchta yanked off her black dress and joined the villagers as they circled the fire. In the ruddy

---

[5] Come to me, my love.
[6] We must light the bonfire and dance!

light of the flames, the naked witch hopped and twirled, her empty breasts flapping against her bony chest. But Bill still only saw the enchanting young woman who had bewitched him. He had no choice but to mindlessly watch her monstrous Danse Macabre[7].

Suddenly, the dancing stopped. Standing on the opposite side of the fire from Bill, Perchta's naked body was clearly visible through the flickering flames. She held out bony arms and called to him, "*Komm zu mir, Liebchen! Komm zu mir!*"[8]

Bill could only obey. Slowly, he took one step toward Perchta and felt the inviting warmth of the fire. He took a second step, and his face began to sweat. After his third step, his clothes started to steam. His fourth step should have caused a burning pain, but he only felt a pleasant warmth. All he could think of was the beautiful naked woman who called to him.

Suddenly, Perchta heard a fast-approaching car. Bursting into the clearing, it struck several of the villagers, who dissolved into mist only to reform into decaying bodies once the car had passed.

Pulling to a stop next to Bill, she jumped out of the car, raced to her husband, and yanked him back from the fire. Before Perchta could react, Sophie hung the second crucifix around Bill's neck, and the witch's spell was broken.

---

[7] French for dance of death.
[8] Come to me, my love. Come to me.

Hexendorf

Awakening as if from a pleasurable dream into a living nightmare, he stared at the witch in confused horror.

"Bill, we have to go!" Sophie yelled. But when they turned, the naked Perchta stood between them and their car.

"*Nein! Er gehört zu mir!*"[9] the witch cried, pointing first at Bill and then at herself.

"Never!" Sophie yelled back, stepping in front of Bill. "He's my husband, witch! Not yours!"

Perchta took a step towards Bill and Sophie. But when the witch saw the two large crucifixes around their necks, she stopped and hissed at them as if she were an enormous snake. Frustrated, she pointed at the couple's car and yelled, "*Feuer!*"

The car instantly burst into flames, forcing Bill and Sophie to back away. The gas tank exploded, and the pair turned to run back down the dirt road leading out of the village.

But Perchta pointed at Bill and Sophie and yelled, "*Greifen sie an!*"[10] With their arms outstretched to capture the couple, the villagers surged forward to surround them.

"I hope this works," Sophie said as she took the bottle of holy water out of her coat pocket. She pulled off its cork and sprayed the water in a wide arc. The instant it touched the villagers

---

[9] No! He belongs to me!
[10] Grab them!

blocking their escape, the holy water broke Perchta's spell, and the affected villagers dissolved into mist. Gritting her teeth, Sophie pulled Bill through the icy fog, and they fled down the path. Hearing the witch and the remaining villagers running right behind them, Bill and Sophie were terrified that at any second, they would feel bony fingers grasping at their backs.

Bill and Sophie didn't stop until they had left the forest, crossed the farmer's field, and reached the road. Looking back, they could see Perchta's barely discernable silhouette in the deep shadows under the trees.

"*Ich verfluche euch beide zur Hölle!*"[11] the witch yelled. Then she turned back toward the village and vanished into the darkness beneath the trees.

"What did the bitch say?" Sophie asked.

"She cursed us to hell," Bill replied. "Do you think she can do that?"

Sophie thought for a second and answered, "I don't think so. They didn't follow us into the farmer's field. I think that means her powers are restricted to Hexendorf and the surrounding woods. And when the sun rises, Hexendorf will vanish for another fifty years."

"So, what do we do now?" Bill asked.

"We walk back to the gasthaus and try to come up with a plausible explanation for what happened to our rental car."

---

[11] I curse you both to Hell!

Hexendorf

Author's Comments

In this short story, I attempted to provide a new and more sinister take on the idea of Brigadoon, a village trapped in time that is only accessible for a single day once every large number of years. In Germany and Austria, Frau Perchta was (among other things) a witch who led lost souls through the air as part of the Wild Hunt and would use her knife to slice open the belly of anyone who crossed her.

REVENGE

It was midnight, and Brad Johnson had just finished his eight-hour swing shift at the Forest Glen Sawmill turning the local trees into lumber. He was bone-tired, sweaty, and wanted nothing more than to get home, take a quick shower, and go to sleep.

A cold rain was pouring down as Johnson walked out to his old pickup truck. After starting the engine, he turned on the windshield wipers, but they left wide streaks of water on the glass. He sighed, silently cursing himself for not replacing the worn-out blades sooner. Ever since the night he had missed a turn and totaled his previous car by running it into a tree, he'd hated driving in the rain after dark. He promised himself to buy new wiper blades first thing after breakfast.

Johnson turned on the radio to his favorite country western music station, pulled out of the parking lot, and headed down the deserted mountain road toward home. His headlights did little to illuminate the thick virgin forest that crowded both sides of the narrow two-lane road.

Johnson yawned, closing his eyes for only an instant, and nearly failed to notice the woman standing at the side of the road. He swerved, skidding to a stop just in time to avoid running into her. Rolling down the passenger side window, he intended to give her a piece of his mind about wearing dark clothes while walking along a road at night. But he held his tongue when he saw she was young and beautiful.

Then Johnson noticed her ripped blouse and the bruises on her face and neck. "Are you all right, miss?"

She shook her head and began to cry.

"You'd better get in out of the rain, and I'll drive you home."

She looked at him fearfully before answering. "I don't know you."

"I'm Brad Johnson, and I live at the mobile home park a few miles up the road. What's your name?"

"Candy. Candy Crawford. I live back in Forest Glen," she said, pointing in the direction from which he had come.

"Well, Candy, now that we know each other, get in so I can drive you home. You can't just stand out here in the rain. Besides, Forest Glen's a good twelve miles from here. It's too far to walk."

Once Candy had opened the door, sat down, and buckled herself in, Johnson turned his pickup around and headed back toward the small town she called home.

"You want to tell me why you're out here all alone in the middle of nowhere?"

"No!"

"Okay," he said, taken aback by the intense anger of her reply. "You don't have to talk about it if you don't want to." He briefly glanced over at her, and for the briefest of moments, his eyes dipped down at the cleavage exposed by her torn blouse.

"You men are all the same!" she exclaimed angrily. "You get a girl alone in your car late at night, and you think she owes you for giving her a ride. You think you can do whatever you want with her."

Shocked at her outburst, Johnson was about to apologize when she suddenly grabbed the top of the steering wheel and yanked it toward her. The pickup swerved to the right, ran off the road, and shot between two trees before crashing into a third. Johnson, who wasn't buckled in, flew forward, smashing his head into the windshield and ramming his chest on the steering wheel.

Candy, however, was unhurt. Before the dazed driver could react, she pulled a small knife from her purse and slashed it across Johnson's throat. Then she calmly wiped the bloody blade on his pants leg, opened her door, and stepped out into the rain. She turned and smiled as she silently stared at the doomed man slowly bleed to death.

With her night's work done, Candy slowly walked back along the road. She had exacted revenge on one more man she was sure was an animal like the one who had raped and strangled her, leaving her dead and battered body in the bushes beside the same road where she took her victims.

A vehicle's headlights appeared in the distance. The black SUV slowed to a stop next to her, and

Revenge

its side window rolled down. Looking in, she saw a man in his mid-fifties with hair and a beard as black as coal.

"You look like you're in trouble," a deep voice said. "Can I give you a ride?"

He smiled at her, though she noticed the smile didn't reach his steely eyes. Looking forward to her second kill of the night, Candy smiled back at the man, who didn't even try to hide that he was leering hungrily at her cleavage.

Opening the door, she sat down next to him. Soon, they were moving far too fast for such a winding road in the middle of a rainy night. Candy didn't mind. No car crash could harm her body, for it was formed not from fragile flesh but from her soul made solid by her hunger for revenge.

"Candy Crawford, we meet at last," the man said. His gravelly voice sounded as if he had smoked a million cigars.

"What? How do you know my name?" she asked, unsettled by the man's unexpected knowledge.

"Oh, I know all about you and your little late-night escapades. How was Brad Johnson? Did you know the innocent man you murdered had a wife and two children? No, of course, not." He chuckled mirthlessly. "You enjoyed watching him die. But killing him didn't satisfy your hunger, did it? You even thought you could do the same thing to me."

Beginning to panic, Candy reached over and grabbed the steering wheel, but the man's grip was like a vise.

"Stop this car and let me out!" she demanded.

"No. I think not."

She tried to open her door to jump out, but the man had locked it.

"There is no escape, Candy. Not tonight, and not from me. It's time you finally pay for your sins."

As she looked on with horror, the man transformed, revealing his true appearance. His clothes disappeared, and his body changed. His skin turned a deep red, and his fingernails turned into claws. His teeth became large and triangular like a shark's, and two short horns grew from his temples.

"I am Andromalius, Hell's high demon in charge of murderers. You're coming with me, my dear. I have a special cell waiting for you."

Andromalius snapped his fingers, and suddenly, they were no longer in the car. Instead, Candy found herself standing next to the demon in a stone hallway that seemingly extended to infinity. Torches burned above each of the thousands of doors that lined the corridor, and the combined heat from their flames made the place feel like the inside of an oven. And the resulting smoke stunk with the stench of sulfur.

Andromalius pointed at the iron bars forming one cell's door. "This small chamber is your new home, and once you enter it, you will never leave. Gaze now upon the man with whom you shall spend eternity."

Candy looked through the bars. "You!" she hissed. Behind the door stood a gaunt man wearing filthy rags that had once been a prison inmate's clothes.

"Poetic, isn't it?" Andromalius observed. "Say hello to Samuel Withers. I'm glad to see you remember him from the night he raped and murdered you. While you've haunted the road where he dumped your body, murdering innocent men to take revenge for what Withers did to you, he was arrested, tried, and sentenced to death by lethal injection. Far too painless a punishment, don't you agree?"

"Damn you, demon!" Withers shouted. "Get on with it!"

"Silence, maggot!" Andromalius commanded, before turning back to Candy. "You must forgive Withers. He's been locked in there ever since his execution. I thought the extra time would make your reunion all the sweeter, so I kept him waiting several decades for this day. You see, Candy, he blames you for his death, just like you blame him for yours. And now the both of you will have all eternity in which to exact your revenge."

The cell door swung open, and Andromalius shoved Candy inside. The door clanged shut behind her with the finality of the grave. A jagged dagger appeared in her hand, and she looked up to see her rapist holding an identical blade.

A Cauldron of Uncanny Dreams

"Stab and slice each other," the demon commanded. "Cut and carve away to your heart's content. Make each other bleed and scream with pain. But know this, you worthless maggots. No wound, no matter how deep, can kill those who are already dead."

And with those words, Andromalius turned and walked away. Hearing the screams from the cell behind him, he paused briefly and smiled. Then he snapped his fingers and disappeared. He had souls to collect, and his work would never end, for Hell would always have empty cells to fill.

Author's Comments

Late one rainy night, a man driving down a deserted road happens upon a woman standing alone in the darkness. What could possibly go wrong?

THE VOW

He must no longer be nor ever have been
Who challenged the Gods with his infernal sin
To raise up the Beast from the dark depths of Hell,
To set the Beast free from its ancient, locked cell,
With powers arcane, and with spells most unclean,
From books and from scrolls that are best left unseen.
Now he must die, his memory be erased,
The Beast be rebound, in its cell be replaced.
To do this we must, and our vow we must keep
So, with order restored, we, at last, may sleep.

Author's Comments

The Vow. In H.P. Lovecraft's "The Case of Charles Dexter Ward," one of Ward's ancestors summoned an unholy power to obtain immortality. The frightened townspeople not only killed the sorcerer, but they also did their best to destroy all memories of the evil man. The idea of going beyond killing the man to killing his memory intrigued me and led me to write "The Vow."

A Cauldron of Uncanny Dreams

HOMAGE TO H. P. LOVECRAFT

The bleak Victorian manor towered above the nearby houses like some eldritch temple of an old forgotten god. Whispered rumors of unholy ceremonies, arcane rites, and barely heard screams had spread far and wide so that few dared to tread the short walk up to that cursed edifice. As the cold and cloudless night fell, an evil miasma of darkness and despair rose from the surrounding grounds. The ghostly mist drifted like a spectral shroud while naked trees raised their skeletal arms into the moonless sky. Strange unnatural creatures, each carrying the captive soul of an innocent child, stalked the town's labyrinthine streets. Driven by hunger and greed, they converged on the master's uncanny abode. Slowly, silently, they crept as lowly supplicants up to that dreadful doorway through which they heard unearthly music, tortured screams, and the rattling of heavy chains. The hideous creatures paused, torn between their hunger and fear. Seconds passed before the bravest stepped forward and struck the massive oaken door with its clawed fist. Once, twice, three times, it pounded. Soon, heavy footsteps approached, and the door creaked open. As one, the creatures intoned the ancient incantation, "Trick-or-treat!"

Homage to H. P. Lovecraft

Author's Comments

As Halloween approached, I thought it fun to do a little homage to H. P. Lovecraft's unique writing style.

AFTERWORD

During October 2020, I was totally occupied with preparing *Hell Holes 3: To Hell and Back* for publication and working with my narrator on the audiobook versions of *Hell Holes 1: What Lurks Below* and *Hell Holes 2: Demons on the Dalton*. Unfortunately, this forced me to wait until now to create this anthology of short stories for Halloween.

Afterword

ACKNOWLEDGMENTS

First, a huge thank you goes to my beta readers, who found numerous places where I could improve the manuscript: Val Ackroyd, Anna Bengtsson, Margaret Bentley, Brandon Cooper, Ann Daniel, Ann Keeran, Sally Kinkade, Barton Paul Levenson, G. McCormick, Margaret Osburn, Mary Popeck, Christie Schneider, Walter Scott, and Julie Wyant.

I initially edited the manuscript for this book using AutoCrit™, Grammarly™, and ProWriting-Aid™. These editing tools found numerous issues to address and correct. Interestingly, each of these tools found problems that the others did not so I feel it was worthwhile to use more than just one of them.

Pamela C. Rice took my initial cover design and gave it a professional flare.

A THANK YOU TO MY READERS

Thank you for purchasing and reading *A Cauldron of Uncanny Dreams*. I hope you enjoyed it and are looking forward to reading other books of mine.

Please Leave an Honest Review

The success of all books, especially books by new Indie authors, greatly depends on their readers. Potential new readers are unlikely to become aware of, let alone purchase, books without sufficient reviews and word-of-mouth recommendations. If you liked this book, please help others enjoy it by recommending it to your friends, both directly and via social media, and by taking a few minutes to write a review at your favorite online bookstore and Goodreads.

If you post an honest book review, please email me at donfiresmith@gmail.com with a link to the review. To show my appreciation, I will send you a coupon for a free ebook copy of the next book I write once it is completed.

OTHER BOOKS BY DONALD FIRESMITH

Fiction

Future Dreams and Nightmares
Hell Holes 1: What Lurks Below
Hell Holes 2: Demons on the Dalton
Hell Holes 3: To Hell and Back
Hell Holes 4: A Slave's Revenge
Magical Wands: A Cornucopia of Wand Lore
The Secrets of Hawthorne House

Nonfiction

The Simulation Theory of Consciousness: or Your Autonomous Car is Sentient
Common Testing Pitfalls and Ways to Prevent and Mitigate Them
The Method Framework for Engineering System Architectures
The OPEN Process Framework
The OPEN Modeling Language (OML) Reference Manual
Documenting a Complete Java Application using OPEN
Dictionary of Object Technology

A Cauldron of Uncanny Dreams

Object-Oriented Analysis and Logical Design

ABOUT THE AUTHOR

Donald Firesmith is a multi-award-winning author of speculative fiction, which includes science fiction (alien invasion), fantasy (magical wands), and modern urban paranormal novels.

Before retiring to devote himself full-time to his novels, Donald Firesmith earned an international reputation as a distinguished engineer, authoring seven system/software engineering books based on his 40+ years spent developing large, complex software-intensive systems.

In addition to reading all manner of books, he relaxes by handcrafting magic wands from various magical woods and mystical gemstones. He lives in Crafton, Pennsylvania, with his wife Becky and various numbers of dogs and cats.

Learn more at his author's website:

https://donaldfiresmith.com

Made in the USA
Monee, IL
03 May 2024